"Does that reassu...

No! she wanted to shout. *...about this insane idea rea...*

But what was the point of saying that? Of course the idea was insane and absurd and outrageous—but Anatole Telonidis was taking it seriously. Talking about it as if it were really going to happen.

Am I really going to go through with this? Go through with a marriage to a man I never knew existed forty-eight hours ago?

A man she was a million miles removed from—a man who lived in the distant stratosphere of the rich, while she was an impecunious student struggling along the breadline.

"Lyn?" His deep, accented voice interrupted her troubled emotions. She jerked her head up and felt the impact of his gaze, felt the flurry in her veins that came as his eyes rested on her, his look enquiring.

"Are we agreed?" he asked.

She bit her lip. She wanted time—time to think, to focus! But how would that help? The longer she delayed, prevaricated, the more likely Anatole Telonidis would get impatient and set his lawyers on to the task of making a formal application to adopt Georgy himself. She took a breath, ragged and uneven.

"Okay," she said. "Okay, I'll do it."

All about the author...
Julia James

JULIA JAMES lives in England with her family. Harlequin® novels were Julia's first "grown-up" books she read as a teenager ("alongside Georgette Heyer and Daphne du Maurier"), and she's been reading them ever since.

Julia adores the English countryside ("and the Celtic countryside!"), in all its seasons, and is fascinated by all things historical, from castles to cottages. She also has a special love for the Mediterranean ("the most perfect landscape after England!")—she considers both ideal settings for romance stories. Since becoming a romance writer, she has, she says, had the great good fortune to start discovering the Caribbean, as well, and is happy to report that those magical, beautiful islands are also ideal settings for romance stories! "One of the best things about writing romance is that it gives you a great excuse to take holidays in fabulous places," says Julia. "All in the name of research, of course!"

In between writing, Julia enjoys walking, gardening, needlework and baking "extremely gooey chocolate cakes"—and trying to stay fit!

Other titles by Julia James available in ebook:

Julia James

Securing the Greek's Legacy

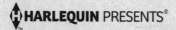

HARLEQUIN PRESENTS®

Recycling programs
for this product may
not exist in your area.

ISBN-13: 978-0-373-13218-8

SECURING THE GREEK'S LEGACY

First North American Publication 2014

Printed in U.S.A.

Securing the Greek's Legacy

For Franny, my dearest friend, in her brave fight against cancer—a fight shared by so many.

CHAPTER ONE

ANATOLE TELONIDIS STARED bleakly across the large, expensively furnished lounge of the penthouse apartment in the most fashionable part of Athens. It was still as untidy as it had been when his young cousin Marcos Petranakos had last walked out of it a few short nightmare weeks ago, straight to his death.

When their mutual grandfather, Timon Petranakos, had phoned his older grandson he had been distraught. *'Anatole, he's dead! Marcos, my beloved Marcos—he's dead!'* the old man had cried out.

Smashed to pieces at twenty-five, driving far too fast in the lethal supercar that had been Timon's own present to Marcos, given in the wake of their grandfather's recent diagnosis with cancer.

The death of his favourite grandson, whom he had spoiled lavishly since Marcos had lost his parents as a teenager, had been a devastating blow. Timon had since refused all treatment for his cancer, longing now only for his own death.

Anatole could understand his grandfather's devastation, his mind-numbing grief. But the fallout from Marcos's tragic death would affect more lives than their own family's. With no direct heir now to the vast Petranakos Corporation, the company would pass to an obscure Petranakos relative whose business inexperience would surely, in these parlous economic times, lead inevitably to the company's collapse and the loss of thousands of jobs, adding to the country's sky-high unemployment levels.

Though Anatole had his own late father's business empire to run—which he did with tireless efficiency and a pressing sense of responsibility—he knew that, had Marcos lived, he could have instilled a similar sense of responsibility into his hedonistic young cousin, guiding him effectively. But the new heir—middle-aged, self-important and conceited—was resistant to any such guidance.

Frustration with the fate awaiting the Petranakos Corporation—and its hapless workforce—Anatole started on the grim process of sorting out his young cousin's possessions. Bleakly, he began his sombre task.

Paperwork was the first essential. As he located Marcos's desk and set about methodically sorting out its jumbled contents a familiar ripple of irritation went through him. Marcos had been the least organised person he'd known—receipts, bills and personal correspondence were all muddled up, demonstrating just how uninterested Marcos had been in anything other than having a good time. Fast cars, high living and an endless procession of highly temporary females had been his favoured lifestyle. Unlike Anatole himself. Running the Telonidis businesses kept him too occupied for anything more than occasional relationships, usually with busy, high-powered businesswomen he worked with in the world of finance.

Frustration bit at Anatole.

If only Marcos had married! Then there might have been a son to inherit from Timon! I'd have kept the Petranakos Corporation safe for him until the child grew up!

But to the fun-seeking Marcos marriage would have been anathema! Girls had been for casual relationships only. There'd be time later for getting married, he'd always said.

But there was to be no later...

Grim-faced, his honed features starkly etched, Anatole went on sorting through the papers in his cousin's desk. Official in one pile, personal in another. The latter pile was not large—not in this age of texting and the internet—but one drawer revealed a batch of three or four envelopes addressed to Marcos in cursive Roman script with a London postmark and UK stamps. Only one had been opened.

Anatole frowned. The lilac-coloured envelopes and the large, looping script suggested a female writer. Though Marcos's dramatic death had been splashed across the Greek tabloids, a British girlfriend might not have heard of it. It might be necessary, Anatole thought reluctantly, for him to let her know of Marcos's fate. That said, he realised as he glanced at the envelopes' postmarks, none of these was dated more recently than nine months ago. Whoever she was, the affair—or whatever it had been— was clearly long over.

With a swift impatience to be done with the whole grim business of sorting through Marcos's personal effects Anatole took the folded single piece of paper from the one envelope that was open. He flicked open the note and started to read the English writing.

And as he did he froze completely...

Lyn made her way out of the lecture hall and sighed. It was no good, she would far rather be studying history! But accountancy would enable her to earn a decent living in the future and that was essential—especially if she were to persuade the authorities that she was capable of raising a child on her own: her beloved Georgy. But for now, while she was still waiting so anxiously to learn if she could adopt him, she was only allowed to be his foster carer. She knew the welfare authorities would prefer for him to be adopted by one of the many childless couples anxious to adopt a healthy baby, but Lyn was determined that no one would take Georgy from her! *No one!*

It didn't matter how much of a struggle it was to keep at her studies while looking after a baby as well, especially with money so short—she would manage somehow! A familiar regret swept over her: if only she'd gone to college sooner and already had her qualifications. But she hadn't been able to go straight from school because she'd had to stay home and look after Lindy. She hadn't been able to leave her young teenage sister to the indifference and neglect which was all her mother had offered. But when Lindy had left school herself and gone to London, to live with a girlfriend and get a job, her mother had been taken ill, her lungs and liver finally giving in after decades of abuse from smoking and alcohol, and there had been no one else to look after her except Lyn.

And now there was Georgy...

'Lyn Brandon?'

It was one of the university's admin staff.

'Someone's asking to see you,' the woman said briskly, and pointed to one of the offices across the corridor.

Frowning, Lyn walked inside.

And stopped dead.

Standing by the window, silhouetted by the fading light, was an imposing, dark-suited figure. Tall, wearing a black cashmere overcoat with a black cashmere scarf hooked around the strong column of his neck, the man had a natural Mediterranean tan that, along with his raven-dark hair, instantly told Lyn that he was not English. Just as the planes and features of his face told her that he was jaw-droppingly good-looking.

It was a face, though, that was staring at her with a mouth set in a tight line—as though he were seeing someone he had not expected. A frown creased his brow.

'Miss Brandon?' He said her name, his voice accented, as if he did not quite believe it.

Dark eyes flicked over her and Lyn felt two spots of colour mount in her cheeks. Immediately she became conscious of the way her hair was caught back in a stringy ponytail. She had not a scrap of make-up on, and her clothes were serviceable rather than fashionable.

Then suddenly, overriding that painful consciousness, there came a jolt of realisation as to just who this clearly foreign man must be—could only be…

The Mediterranean looks, the expensive clothes, the sleekly groomed looks, the whole aura of wealth about him… She felt her stomach constrict, filling with instinctive fear.

Across the narrow room Anatole caught the flash of alarm and wondered at it, but not nearly as much as he was wondering whether he had, after all, really tracked down the woman he'd been so urgently seeking ever since reading that letter in Marcos's apartment—the woman who, so his investigators had discovered, had most definitely given birth to a baby boy…

Is he Marcos's son? The question was burning in hope. Because if Marcos had had a son then it changed everything. *Everything!*

If, by a miracle, Marcos had a son, then Anatole had to find him and bring him home to Greece, so that Timon, who was fading with every passing day, could find instead a last blessing from the cruel fate that had taken so much from him.

And it was not just for his grandfather that a son of Marcos's would be a blessing, either, Anatole knew. This would persuade Timon to change his will, to acknowledge that his beloved Marcos had had a son to whom he could now leave the Petranakos Corporation. Infant though he was, Anatole would guard the child's inheritance, keep it safe and prosperous for him—and save the livelihoods of all its employees.

Tracking down the author of the letters had led him first to a council house in the south of the country and then, through information given to his detectives by neighbours, to this northern college, where he'd been told the young woman he was so urgently seeking—Linda Brandon— had recently moved.

But as his eyes rested now on the woman he was addressing he felt doubt fill him. *This* was the woman he'd trekked to this grim, rainswept northern town to find in a race against time for his stricken grandfather? Marcos wouldn't even have looked twice at her—let alone taken her to his bed!

'*Are* you Miss Brandon?' he asked, his voice sharper now.

He saw her swallow and nod jerkily. Saw, too, that her entire body had tensed.

'I am Anatole Telonidis,' he announced. His voice sounded clipped, but his mission was a painful one—and an urgent one. 'I am here on behalf of my cousin, Marcos Petranakos, with whom I believe you are…' he sought the right phrase '…acquainted.'

Even as he said it his eyes flicked over her again doubtfully. Even putting aside her unprepossessing appearance, Marcos's taste had been for curvy blondes—not thin brunettes. But her reaction told him that she must indeed be the person he was looking for so urgently—she had instantly recognised Marcos's name.

And not favourably…

Her expression had changed. Hardened. 'So he couldn't even be bothered to come himself!' she retorted scornfully.

If she'd sought to hit home with her accusation she'd failed. The man who'd declared himself Marcos Petranakos's cousin stilled. In the dark eyes a flash of deep emotion showed and Lyn saw his face stiffen.

'The situation is not as you suppose,' he said.

It was as if, she realised, he was picking his words carefully.

He paused a moment, as if steeling himself to speak, then said, 'I must talk to you. But the matter is…difficult.'

Lyn shook her head violently. She could feel the adrenaline running through her body. 'No, it's not difficult at all!' she retorted. 'Whatever message you've been sent to deliver by your cousin, you needn't bother! Georgy—his *son*!—is fine without him. Absolutely fine!'

She saw emotion flash in his dark eyes again, saw the shadow behind it. Out of nowhere a chill went through her.

'There is something I must tell you,' Anatole Telonidis was saying. His voice was grim, and bleak, as if he were forcing the words out.

Lyn's hands clenched. 'There is nothing you can say that I care about—!' she began.

But his deep, sombre voice cut right through hers. 'My cousin is dead.'

There was silence. Complete silence. Wordlessly, Anatole cursed himself for his blunt outburst. But it had been impossible to hear her hostility, her scorn, when Marcos lay dead in his grave…

'Dead?' Lyn's voice was hollow with shock.

'I'm sorry. I should not have told you so brutally,' Anatole said stiffly.

She was still staring at him. 'Marcos Petranakos is *dead*?' Her voice was thin—disbelieving.

'It was a car crash. Two months ago. It has taken time to track you down…' His words were staccato, sombre.

Lyn swayed as if she might pass out. Instantly Anatole was there, catching her arm, staying her. She stepped back, steadying herself, and he released her. Absently she noticed with complete irrelevance how strong his grasp had been. How overpowering his momentary closeness.

'He's dead?' she said again, her voice hollow. Emotion twisted in her throat. Georgy's father was dead…

'Please,' Anatole Telonidis was saying, 'you need to sit down. I am sorry this is such a shock to you. I know,' he went on, picking his words carefully again, she could tell, his expression guarded, 'just how…deep…you felt the relationship was between yourself and him, but—'

A noise came from her. He stopped. She was staring at him, but the expression in her face was different now, Anatole registered. It wasn't shock at hearing about Marcos's tragic death. It wasn't even anger—the understandable anger, painful though it was for him to face it—that she'd expressed about the man who had got her pregnant and then totally ignored her ever since.

'Between him and *me*?' she echoed. She shook her head a moment, as if clearing it.

'Yes,' Anatole pursued. 'I know from your letters—which, forgive me, I have read—that you felt a strong… attachment to my cousin. That you were expressing your longing to…' He hesitated, recalling vividly the hopelessly optimistic expectations with which she had surrounded her announcement that she was carrying Marcos's baby. 'Your longing to make a family together, but—'

He got no further.

'I'm not Georgy's mother,' Lyn announced.

And in her bleak voice were a thousand unshed tears.

For a moment Anatole thought he had not heard correctly. Or had misunderstood what she had said in English. Then his eyes levelled on hers and he realised he had understood her exactly.

'What?' His exclamation was like a bullet. A blackening frown sliced down over his face. 'You said you were Linda Brandon!' he threw at her accusingly.

His thoughts were in turmoil. What the hell was going on? He could make no sense of it! He could see her shaking her head—a jerky gesture. Then she spoke, her voice strained.

'I'm…I'm Lynette Brandon,' Anatole heard her say.

He saw her take a rasping breath, making herself speak. Her face was still white with shock with what he'd told her about Marcos.

'Lindy…Linda—' she gave her sister's full name before stopping abruptly, her voice cutting off. Then she blinked.

Anatole could see the shimmer of tears clearly now.

'Linda was my sister,' she finished, her voice no more than a husk.

He heard the past tense—felt the slow, heavy pulse of dark realisation go through him. Heard her thin, shaky voice continuing, telling him what was so unbearably painful for her to say.

Her face was breaking up.

'She died,' she whispered. 'My sister Linda. Georgy's mother. She died giving birth. Eclampsia. It's not supposed to happen any more. But it did…*it did*…'

Her voice was broken.

She lifted her eyes to Anatole across a divide that was like a yawning chasm—a chasm that had claimed two young lives.

Her mind reeled as she took in the enormity of the truth they had both revealed to each other. The unbearable tragedy of it.

Both Georgy's parents were dead!

She had thrown at Anatole Telonidis the fact that his uncaring, irresponsible cousin wasn't wanted or needed by his son, but to hear that he had suffered the same dreadful fate as her sister was unbearable. As unbearable as losing her sister had been. Tears stung in her eyes and his voice came from very far away.

'You should sit down,' said Anatole Telonidis.

He guided her to a chair and she sat on it nervelessly. His own mind was still reeling, still trying to come to grips with what he had just learnt. The double tragedy surrounding Marcos's baby son.

Where was he? Where was Marcos's son?

That was the question he had to have answered now! A cold fear went through him. Newborn babies were in high demand for adoption by childless couples, and a fatherless baby whose mother had died in childbirth might have been just such a child...

Had he been adopted already? The question seared in Anatole's head. If so, then he would have a nightmare of a search to track him down—even if he were allowed to by the authorities. And if he had already been adopted then would his adoptive parents be likely to let him go? Would the authorities be likely to let him demand—*plead*!—that they accede to his need for Timon to know that he had an heir after all?

He stood looking down at the sister of the woman who had borne his cousin a child and died in the process. He swallowed.

'Where is my cousin's son?' he asked. He tried not to sound brusque, demanding, but he had to know. *He had to know!*

Her chin lifted, her eyes flashing to his.

'He's with *me*!' came the answer. Vehement, passionate.

Abstractedly Anatole found himself registering that when this drab dab of a female spoke passionately her nondescript features suddenly sharpened into life, giving her a vividness that was not drab at all. Then the sense of her words hit him.

'With *you*?'

She took a ragged breath, her fingers clutching the side

of the chair. 'Yes! With me! And he's staying with me! That's all you need to know!'

She leapt to her feet, fear and panic impelling her. Too much had happened—shock after shock—and she couldn't cope with it, couldn't take it in.

Anatole stepped towards her, urgency in his voice. 'Miss Brandon, we have to talk—discuss—'

'No! There's nothing to discuss! *Nothing!*'

And then, before his frustrated gaze, she rushed from the room.

Lyn fled. Her mind was in turmoil. Though she managed to make her way into her next lecture she was incapable of concentrating. Only one single emotion was uppermost.

Georgy is mine! Mine, mine, mine!

Lindy had given the baby to her with her dying breath and she would *never*, never betray that! *Never!*

Grief clutched at Lyn again.

'Look after Georgy—'

They had been Lindy's final words before the darkness had closed over her fevered, stricken brain and she had ebbed from life.

And I will! I will look after him all my life—all his life— and I will never let any harm come to him, never abandon him or give up him!

'Just you and me, Georgy!' she whispered later as, morning lectures finally over, she collected him from the college crèche and made her way to the bus stop and back home for the afternoon.

But as she clambered on board the bus, stashing the folding buggy one-handed as she held Georgy in the other, she completely failed to see an anonymous black car pull out into the road behind the bus. Following it.

Two hours later Anatole stood in front of the block of flats his investigator had informed him was Lynette Brandon's place of accommodation and stared bleakly at it. It was not an attractive building, being of ugly sixties design, with stained concrete and peeling paint. The whole area was just as dreary—no place for Timon Petranakos's great-grandson to be brought up!

Resolve steeling, he rang the doorbell.

CHAPTER TWO

Lyn had sat down at the rickety table in the corner of the living room and got out her study books. Georgy had been fed and changed, and had settled for his afternoon nap in his secondhand cot, tucked in beside her bed in the single bedroom the flat possessed. She was grateful for Georgy's afternoon sleep, even though if he slept too much he didn't sleep well at night, for it gave her an hour or two of solid homework time. But today her concentration was shot to pieces—still reeling with what had happened that morning.

Hopefully she had made her position clear and the man who had lobbed a bombshell into her life would take himself off again, back to Greece, and leave her alone. Anxiety rippled through her again. The adoption authorities believed that there was no contact with Georgy's father or any of his paternal family. But since this morning that wasn't true any more...

No, she mustn't think about that! She must put it behind her. Put behind her all the dark, disturbing images of the man whose incredible good looks were such a source of disturbance to her. For a moment his image formed in her mind, overpowering in its masculine impact. She thrust it impatiently aside and started reading her textbook.

Two minutes later she was interrupted. The doorbell had sounded. Imperative. Demanding.

Her head shot up. Who on earth…? No one called on her here.

The bell rang again. Warily, heart thumping suddenly, she went to the door, lifting up the entryphone.

'Who is it?' she asked sharply.

'Miss Brandon—we need to continue our conversation.'

It was Anatole Telonidis.

For a moment Lyn remained motionless. *Don't let him in!* The childish, fearful words sounded in her head, but she knew she could not obey them. She had to get this conversation over and done with. Then she could send him away and never see him again—never be troubled again by the existence of Georgy's father's family. Nervelessly she pressed the entry buzzer, and a few moments later opened her front door.

He was just as tall and formidable as she remembered. Taller, it seemed, in her poky flat. But it was not just his size and demeanour that pressed on her senses. His physical presence was dominating more than just the space he stood in. It was making her horribly aware all over again of his dark, devastating looks.

Desperately she tried to crush down her awareness of them. It was the last thing she should be paying any attention to right now!

Besides, a vicious little voice in her head was reminding her to think about what *he* was seeing! He was seeing a plain-faced nobody who was wearing ancient baggy jeans and a thick frumpy jumper, with her hair tied back and not a scrap of make-up. A man like him wouldn't even look once, let alone twice!

Oh, for God's sake, what are you even thinking of? Focus—just focus! This is about Georgy and what this man wants—or doesn't want.

And how quickly she could get rid of him…

She stared at him. He seemed to be looking about him,

then past her into the small living room, with its shabby furniture, worn carpet and hideously patterned curtains. Her chin went up. Yes, the place was uninviting, but it was cheap, and it came furnished, and she wasn't going to be choosy. She couldn't afford to be—not until she was earning a decent salary. Till then Georgy didn't care that he wasn't anywhere nice. And neither did she.

This man who had dropped a bombshell into her life, however, looked as if he cared—and he didn't like what he was seeing.

'I hope,' he said evenly, 'that you have now had a chance to come to terms with what I told you this morning, and that you understand,' he continued, 'how imperative it is that we discuss my cousin's son's future.'

'There's nothing to discuss,' she replied tightly.

Anatole's mouth tightened. So she was still taking that line. Well, he would have to disabuse her of it—that was all. In the meantime there was something that was even more imperative. He wanted to see Marcos's son—see him with his own eyes. He looked around the room.

'Where is the baby?' he asked. He hadn't meant it to sound like a demand, only a question, but it seemed to make the girl flinch. Seeing her now, like this, had not improved her looks, he noted absently. She was still abysmally dressed, without any attention to her appearance.

'He's asleep,' she answered stiffly.

The dark eyes rested on her. 'I would like to see him.'

It was not a request. It was a statement of intent. His eyes went past her to the half-open bedroom door and he stepped towards it. Inside was a cot beside a bed, and in the cot the small figure of a baby nestled in a fleecy blanket. In the dim light from the drawn curtains Anatole could not make out the baby's features.

Are you Marcos's son? Are you the child I've come to find? The questions burned in his head. Instinctively he moved to step into the room. Immediately a low-voiced hiss sounded behind him.

'Please don't wake him!'

He could hear a note in her voice that was not just a command but a plea. Abruptly, he nodded, reversing out of the cramped room, causing her to back away into the equally small living room.

Once again she felt his presence dominate the poky space.

'You had better sit down, Miss Brandon,' he said, indicating the sofa as though he, not her, was the host.

Stiffly, she did so. Somehow she had to find a way to make him go away—leave her and Georgy alone. Then it came to her just why he might be here. What he might be after.

'If you want me to sign papers saying I forfeit any claim to his father's estate, I will do so straight away,' she blurted out. 'I don't want any money, or maintenance, or anything like that. Georgy and I are fine as we are—we're all sorted!' She swallowed again, altering her tone of voice. Her eyes shadowed suddenly. 'I'm sorry to hear that your cousin is…is dead…but—' her eyes met his unflinchingly '—but it doesn't change the fact that he was not in the slightest bit interested in Georgy's existence, so—'

Anatole Telonidis held up a hand. It was a simple gesture, but it carried with it an expectation that she would cease talking.

Which she did.

'My cousin is…*was*,' he corrected himself painfully, 'the only Petranakos grandson of our mutual grandfather, Timon. Marcos's parents died when he was only a teenager and consequently…' Anatole paused. 'He was very precious to our grandfather. His death has devastated him.' He took another heavy breath. 'Marcos's death came as a viciously cruel blow—he was killed driving the car that our grandfather had given him for his birthday. It was a birthday Timon knew would likely be the last he would see, because...' Anatole paused again, then finished the bleak saga. 'Because Timon had himself just been diagnosed with advanced incurable cancer.'

He fell silent, letting the information sink in. Lynette Brandon was sitting there, looking ashen.

'You will understand, I know,' he went on quietly, 'how much it will mean to Timon to know that, although he has lost his grandson, a great-grandson exists.' He read her expression. It was blank, rejecting. He *had* to convince her of the argument he was making. 'There is very little time,' he pressed. 'The cancer was very advanced at the point of diagnosis, and since my cousin's death my grandfather has refused all treatment—even though treatment could keep him alive for a little while longer. He is waiting to die—for with the loss of his grandson he has no reason to live at all. Not even for one single day.' Then he finished what he had come to say. 'Your sister's baby—my cousin's son—gives him that reason.'

He stood looking down at her. Her face was still ashen, her hands twisting in her lap. He spoke again, his voice grave. He had to convince her of the urgency of what had to happen.

'I need to take Georgy to Greece with me. I need to take him as soon as possible. My dying grandfather needs to know that his great-grandson will grow up in the country of his father—'

'*No!* No, I won't let you!' The words burst from her and she leapt to her feet.

Anatole pressed his lips together in frustration. 'You are overwrought,' he repeated. 'It is understandable—this has come as a shock to you. I wish that matters were not as urgent as they are. But with Timon's state of health I have to press you on this! The very last thing I want,' he said heavily, 'is to turn this into any kind of battle between us.

I need—I *want*—your co-operation! You do not need me to tell you,' he added, and his eyes were dark now, 'that once DNA testing has proved Marcos's paternity, then—'

'There isn't going to *be* any DNA testing!' Lyn shot back at him.

Anatole stopped. There was something in her voice—something in her face—that alerted him. There was more than obduracy in it—more than anger, even.

There was fear.

His antennae went into overdrive. *Thee mou*, might the child not be Marcos's after all? Everything about those plaintive, pitiful letters he'd read indicated that the baby's mother had been no promiscuous party girl, that she had fallen in love with his cousin, however unwisely. No, the child she had been carrying *was* his. He was certain of it. Timon, he knew, would require proof before he designated the baby his heir, but that would surely be a formality?

His thoughts raced back to the moment in hand. The expression on Lynette Brandon's face made no sense. She was the one objecting to any idea of taking Marcos's son back to Greece—if the baby were not Marcos's after all surely she would positively *want* DNA testing done!

He frowned. There was something else that didn't make sense, either. Something odd about her name. Its similarity to her sister's. Abruptly he spoke. 'Why is your sister's name so like yours?' he asked shortly. He frowned. 'It is unusual—confusing, as I have found—for sisters to have such similar names. Lynette and Linda.'

'So what?' she countered belligerently. 'What does it matter now?'

Anatole fixed his gaze on her. His antennae were now registering that same flash of emotion in her as he'd seen when he had mentioned DNA testing, but he had no time to consider it further. Lynette Brandon was launching into him again. Her voice was vehement, passionate.

'Have I finally got you to understand, Mr Telonidis, that your journey here has been wasted? I'm sorry—sorry about your cousin, sorry about your grandfather—but Georgy is staying here with me! He is *not* going to be brought up in Greece. He is *mine*!'

'Is he?'

His brief, blunt question cut right across her. Silencing her.

In her eyes, her face, flared that same emotion he had seen a moment ago—fear.

What is going on here?

The question flared in his head and stayed there, even though her voice broke that moment of silence with a single hissing word.

'*Yes!*' she grated fiercely.

Anatole levelled his gaze at her. Behind his impassive expression his mind was working fast. Since learning that morning about the double tragedy that had hit this infant, overturning his assumption that Marcos's son was with his birth mother, he had set his lawyers to ascertain exactly what the legal situation was with regard to custody of the orphaned boy—and what might be the outcome of any proposition that the baby be raised in Greece by his paternal family. He had no answers yet, but the baby's aunt had constantly—and vehemently!—expressed the fact that *she* had full legal charge in her sister's place.

But *did* she?

'And that is official, is it? Your custody of Georgy?' His voice was incisive, demanding she answer.

Again there was that same revealing emotion in her eyes, which was then instantly blanked.

'*Yes!*' she repeated, just as fiercely.

He frowned. 'So you have adopted him?'

A line of white showed on her cheekbones. 'It's going through,' she said quickly. 'These things take time. There's a lot of paperwork. Bureaucracy and everything. But of *course* I'm adopting him! I'm the obvious person to adopt him!'

His expression did not change, but he could see that for the British authorities she would be the natural person to adopt her late sister's son if she were set on doing so. Which she evidently was! Anatole felt a ripple of respect for her determination to go through with it. Her life could not be easy, juggling studying with childcare and living in penny-pinching circumstances.

But for all that, he still had to find a way to convince her that Marcos's son just could *not* be raised by her in such penurious circumstances. It was unthinkable. Once Timon knew of his existence, he would insist with all his last strength that his beloved grandson's son be brought home to Greece, to be reunited with his father's family.

Just how, precisely, Marcos's son was to be raised—how a small baby, then a toddler and a schoolboy was to grow up—was something that could be worked out later. For now, just getting the baby to Greece, for his grandfather to see him—make him his heir—before the cancer claimed Timon was his only priority.

And to do that he had to get this totally impossible intransigent aunt to stop blocking him at every turn!

But how?

A heavy, unappetising thought forced its way forward. His mouth tightened. There was, of course, one very obvious method of attempting to stop any objections to what he was urging. A way that worked, as he knew well from his own business experience, to win compliance and consensus and agreement.

A way he did not want to use here, now, for this—but if he had to…if it worked…?

He must. If nothing else he must attempt it. He owed it to Timon, to Marcos—to all the thousands employed by the Petranakos Corporation whose livelihoods were threatened.

Reluctantly, for what he was about to say went against the grain, he spoke. His tone of voice was measured, impassive. 'I know full well that Timon will insist on thanking you for your care and concern for his great-grandson—that he will fully appreciate the accommodation you make towards granting his fervent wish for Marcos's son to grow up with his paternal family—and that he will wish to settle a sum on you in respect of his gratitude and appreciation such that your financial security would be handsomely assured for the future.'

There—he had said it. He had said outright that if she stopped stonewalling him her life of poverty would be over for good. He let the words sink in, not taking his eyes from her.

Her expression was blank, however. Had she not heard what he'd said?

Then she answered him. 'You want to *buy* Georgy from me?' Her voice was as blank as her eyes.

A frown immediately shaped Anatole's face. 'Of course not!' he repudiated.

'You're offering me money to hand him over to you,' the same blank voice intoned.

Anatole shook his head. Did she have to put it in such unpalatable terms? 'What I am saying,' he spelt out, 'is that—'

'Is that your grandfather will pay me if I let him have Georgy to bring him up in Greece.' Her voice was flat.

'No! It is not like that—' Anatole's voice was sharp.

Suddenly the blank look in her eyes vanished utterly. She launched herself to her feet, anger blazing in her eyes.

'It is *exactly* like that!' she cried. 'How *dare* you? How dare you sit there and tell me you'll *buy* Georgy from me? How *dare* you do such a thing?' Her voice had risen; her heart was thumping furiously. 'How *dare* you come here and offer me *money* to hand my dead sister's son over to you? How dare you?'

He was on his feet as well. He filled the room, intimidating and overpowering. But she would not be intimidated! Would not be overpowered! Would not be paid to part with Georgy!

She took a heaving breath, words pouring from her.

'I swore to my sister on her *deathbed* that I would never, never abandon her baby! That I would never hand him over to *anyone*! That I would always, *always* look after him and love him. Because she was not going to be able to do it! Because she was dying, and she knew she was dying, and she was never going to see her baby grow up, never going to see him become a boy, a man—never, never, *never…*'

Her voice was hoarse, the words torn from her, from the very depths of her being. Her hands were clenched into fists at her sides, as if she could—and would—and *must*—fight off the whole world to keep Georgy with her!

For a second there was silence. Absolute silence between them. Then into the silence came a high, solitary wail.

With a cry of consternation Lyn wheeled about. Oh, no—now she had gone and woken Georgy! With all this awful arguing about what was never going to happen—because she was never giving Georgy up! *Never!*

The wail came again. She rounded on Anatole. 'Please go!' she said. 'Please—just go!'

She rushed from the room into the bedroom, where Georgy was wide awake, his little face screwed up. She scooped him up with a hushing noise, soothing and rocking him in her arms until he had quietened.

The feel of his strong, solid little body, so familiar, so precious, calmed her too. She took long slow breaths, hugging him tightly, and felt his warmth and weight in her arms like a blessing, a benediction.

How could anyone think to ask her to give him up? She loved this little child more than anyone in the whole world! He was everything to her—and she was everything to him.

Love flowed from her, enveloping and protective, as she cradled him against her, her eyes smarting, her throat tight. Slowly the heaving emotions in her breast, her heart, eased. Georgy was safe. He was in her arms. He was with her. She would never let him go, never abandon him. Her hectic pulse slowed. Cradling him, her hand curved protectively around his back, she crooned soothingly at him, wordless sounds murmuring, familiar and comforting. The rest of the world seemed very far away…

'May I see him?'

The voice behind her made her spin round. Anatole was standing in the doorway of the bedroom.

But there was something different about him. Something quite different. She'd seen him only as dark and tall and formidable—telling her things she did not want to hear, his very presence a terrifying threat to everything that she held most dear.

Now, as she gazed at him, her expression stricken, across the dimly lit curtained room, he did not seem formidable at all. Or threatening. He seemed merely—tense. As if every muscle in his body were pulled taut. In the dim light the bone structure of his face was stark.

She felt Georgy lift his head from her shoulder, twist his neck so that he could see where the voice had come from. He gazed at the figure in the doorway with eyes just as dark as those which were fixed on him.

For a moment the tableau held all of them immobile. Then, with a gurgling sound, Georgy lurched on her shoulder, his little arms reaching forward towards the man standing in the doorway. The man with eyes like his own.

The man who was kin to the father he had never known. Never would know now....

As if in slow motion, Anatole found his hand reaching inside his jacket pocket, drawing out something he had brought with him from Greece. It was a silver photo frame from his grandfather's opulent drawing room, displaying one individual alone. Slowly he shifted his gaze down to the photo he held in his hand, then back to the baby cradled so closely in his young aunt's arms.

'He is Marcos's son.' Anatole's voice was flat. But there was emotion in it. Powerful emotion. His gaze cut suddenly to Lyn. 'Look,' he instructed, holding up the photo.

It was an old one, pre-digital, an informal shot and unposed, but the likeness to the baby in it was unmistakable. The same wide brown-eyed gaze. The same-shaped mouth and head. The same expression.

How was it, Anatole found himself thinking, emotion rising in his chest, that the genes Marcos had carried could be so clearly visible even at this tender age? What was it about the human face that revealed its origins, its kinship? Yet so it was—this scrap of humanity, less than a year old, stared back at him in the baby he himself could just dimly remember from his own boyhood.

'I couldn't be sure,' he heard himself saying. 'Knew that I must get DNA testing. Knew there would be doubts that necessitated such measures.' He paused. 'But I have no doubts—not now.' His voice changed, and so did his expression. 'This is my cousin's son—his *only* son! The only trace left of him in this life! He *must* be part of his father's family.' He held up a hand as if to pre-empt what he knew would be her response to that unarguable statement. 'But we must find a way…there must be one—' He broke off, taking a sharp breath, his focus now on Lyn.

'I am sorry—sorry that I said what I did just now. It

was offensive, and you have every right to be angry.' He paused. 'Will you accept my apology?'

His eyes met hers, seeking a way past the stormy expression in them. Slowly, painfully, Lyn swallowed. There was a large stone in her throat, but it was not only from her anger at his vile offer. It was because of the way he'd stared at Georgy…the emotion in his eyes…his voice.

He was seeing his dead cousin in the baby she was holding in her arms…

Just as I see Lindy in him.

She felt her throat close—felt something change, somehow, deep within her. Slowly she nodded, taking a ragged breath.

'Thank you,' he said in a low voice.

His eyes went from her face back to Georgy. That expression returned to them, making her breath catch as the same emotion was aroused in herself.

Warily Lyn made her way past him into the living room, heading for the sofa onto which she sank down on shaky legs, her heart rate still ragged. But something had changed. She could feel it—sense it as clearly as if the wind had changed its quarter, as if the tide had turned in the depths of the sea. It was in his voice, his stance, his face, as he sat down at the far end of the sofa.

And it was in her, too, that change. Was it because she was finally accepting that Georgy was more than her dead sister's son? That he had a family on his father's side too, to whom he was precious—as precious as he was to her?

She did not want to accept that truth—had tried to fight it—but she had to. Must.

For a moment—just a moment—as Anatole Telonidis lowered his tall frame on to the sofa, he seemed far too physically close to her. She wanted to leap to her feet—away from the intensely physical presence of the man. But even as she fought the impulse she could feel Georgy using his not inconsiderable strength to lean forward, towards this interesting addition to his world. And as he did so, he gave another crowing gurgle, his little arms stretching forward towards his father's cousin.

And then Lyn saw something quite extraordinary happen.

Before her eyes she saw this tall, dark, forbidding man who had walked uninvited into her world, catalysing her deepest fears with his demands, his assumptions, all the power of his wealth and family, transform. Greek words sounded from his mouth and then slowly, as if he were moving through thick, murky water, she watched him reach a hand out towards the infant. Immediately a little starfish fist closed around the long, tanned finger and tugged it hopefully, if ineffectually, in the direction of his mouth.

'Hello, Georgy,' said Anatole. His voice sounded strained, as if his throat weren't working properly. 'Hello, little fellow.'

There was, Lyn could see as plain as day, extraordinary though it was, a look of stunned wonder on his dark, formidable face.

She felt emotion stab at her but did not know what it was. Only that it was powerful. *Very* powerful...

Her eyes could not leave his face, could not stop staring at the transformation in the man. But Anatole had no eyes for her stunned scrutiny of him. He had eyes only for one thing—the baby in her arms who had brought him here. His dead cousin's child.

Lyn heard him murmur something in Greek. Something that sounded soft and caressing. Something that felt like a warm touch on her skin even though it was not directed at her. It drew a response from her, all the same, and she felt a strange, potent flickering of her senses.

Then Georgy was wriggling impatiently in her arms, tugging on the finger he was clutching. She loosened her hold automatically, so that he could gain his objective, but now he had seen something more enticing to clutch, and he dropped the finger he'd been gripping. Instead he made a lunge at the dark silk tie dangling so tantalisingly close to him as its wearer leant forward. To his own considerable pleasure he made contact, grasped it greedily, and pulled the end into his mouth, sucking vigorously.

A burst of laughter broke from Lyn. She couldn't help it. 'Oh, Georgy, you monkey!' she exclaimed ruefully.

She lifted a hand to disengage the tie, conscious as she did so that the gesture brought her disquietingly closer to the man wearing it. Deprived of his tasty morsel, Georgy gave a howl of outrage. Lyn took his tiny hands and busied herself in remonstrations that enabled her to straighten up, increasing the distance between herself and this most disturbing of men.

'No, you can't have it! You little monster, you! Yes, you are! A little monster!' She nuzzled his nose with an Eskimo kiss and set him laughing. She glanced across at Anatole at what was doubtless a hideously expensive tie now somewhat soggy at the end. 'I'm sorry about that. I hope it's not damaged too much.' Her voice was apologetic, constrained with an embarrassment that was not just due to Georgy's misdemeanours but also to the awkward self-consciousness of sharing a sofa with Anatole Telonidis.

Anatole surveyed the soggy item. 'It is of no consequence,' he remarked.

Then, before Lyn realised what he was doing, he was unfastening his gold watch and offering it to Georgy. Eyes widening in disbelieving delight, Georgy snatched up the shiny treasure and clutched it to his chest, gazing wide-eyed at the giver of such largesse.

'You're mad!' exclaimed Lyn, throwing a shocked glance at Anatole. 'He'll try and eat it!'

But Anatole merely looked at the baby. 'Georgy. No eating. A gentleman does not eat his watch. Understood?'

Georgy stared, his eyes wide in wonder. This stern, deep voice had clearly made a deep impression on him. Dutifully, he made no attempt to ingest the Rolex, contenting himself with continuing to clutch it while staring riveted at this oracle of good advice.

Anatole cast a long-lashed sardonic look at Lyn—a strangely intimate glance that sent a quiver through her. Then the next second his moment of triumph evaporated. With a jerky movement Georgy slammed the watch to his mouth.

'Georgy—no!' Both adults moved fast but, alas, Anatole's belated attempt to remove his watch incited outrage in the infant, whose little face screwed up into angry tears.

Hastily Lyn fumbled in the plastic toy bucket beside the sofa to fetch out Georgy's favourite—a set of plastic keys—and managed to swap them, with some difficulty, for the precious gold watch. Charily, she handed the latter back to its owner, avoiding eye contact this time, and then busied herself settling Georgy in her lap as he chewed contentedly on his keys. She felt unbearably awkward, and yet she knew that something had changed. Thawed.

Imperceptibly, she felt a tiny amount of the tension racking her easing. Then, into the brief silence, a deep voice spoke.

'So, what are we to do?'

CHAPTER THREE

LYN'S EYES FLEW upwards. Anatole Telonidis was looking at her, and as he did so she knew for sure that something had definitely changed between them. She was still wary, yes—wariness was prickling through her every vein—but that wash of rage and outrage against him had gone. His tone of voice was different too. It was more—open. As if he were no longer simply dictating to her what must happen. As if he were truly asking a question of her.

A question she could give no answer to other than the one she had hurled at his head five minutes ago. She could not—*would* not—ever give Georgy up!

She gave an awkward shrug, dropping her eyes again. She didn't want to look at him. Her self-consciousness had soared suddenly, and whereas before she might have found refuge in animosity and resentment and rage against him and his autocratic demands, now she felt raw and exposed.

Anatole watched her sitting there, with the baby on her lap, her attention all on the infant who was busily chewing on his keys and chuntering away to himself. Emotion poured through him, powerful and overwhelming. Even without the formality of DNA testing his heart already knew that this was Marcos's son. And already he felt a powerful urge to protect and cherish him.

Which is what she feels too! That is what is driving her!

Her obduracy, her angry outburst, were both fuelled

by the deepest of emotions—emotions that he understood and recognised.

Love and grief.

She could not give up the child. Not now. Not like this. It was impossible for her to conceive of such a thing. Impossible for her to do anything other than what she had done—rage at the very notion of it! A flicker of a different emotion went through him—one he had not envisaged feeling. One that came again now as he let his eyes rest on her while her attention was on the baby in her lap.

There was something very moving about seeing her attend so tenderly to the tiny scrap of humanity she was engaged with. Her face seemed softer somehow, without that pinched, drained, defensive look that he'd seen in it. The contours of her profile, animated by her smiles of affection for the infant, were gentler now.

He found an irrelevant thought fleeting through his head. *If she had her hair done decently, took some trouble over her appearance, she would look quite different—*

He reproached himself. What time or funds did she have to pay any attention to her appearance? She was studying full-time and looking after a baby, on what was clearly a very tight budget. And it was obvious, too, from the circles under her eyes, that she wasn't getting enough sleep.

A sudden impulse went through him.

I could lighten her burden—the load she is carrying single-handed.

But not by taking from her the baby she was so devoted to.

He heard himself speaking. 'There must be a way we can reach agreement.'

Her eyes flew to his. Back in them, he could see, was the wariness and alarm that he was so familiar with.

'You're not taking Georgy from me!' Fear and the hostility raked through her voice, flashed in her eyes.

He held up a hand. His voice changed, grew husky. 'I can see how much Marcos's son means to you. But *because* he means so much to you I ask you to understand how much he means to his father's family as well.' He paused, his eyes holding hers, willing the wariness and resistance to dissolve. 'I need you to trust me,' he said to her. 'I need you to believe me when I say that there has to be a way we can resolve this *impasse*.'

She heard his words. Heard them reach her—strong, fluent, persuasive. Felt the power of that dark, expressive gaze on her, and the power, too, of the magnetism of the man, the power of his presence, the impact it had on her. She felt her senses stir and fought them back. But she could not fight back the intensity of his regard—the way those incredible eyes were holding hers, willing her to accept what he was saying to her.

He pressed on. 'I do not wish,' he said, making his words as clear as he could, 'for there to be animosity or conflict between us. A way can be found. I am sure of it. If...' He paused, and now his eyes were more intense than ever. 'If there is goodwill between us and, most importantly, trust.'

She felt her emotions sway, her resistance weaken.

As if he sensed it, saw it, he went on. 'Will you bring Georgy to Greece?' he asked. 'For a visit—I ask nothing more than that for now,' he emphasized. 'Simply so that his great-grandfather can see him.'

His eyes searched her face. Alarm flared again in her eyes.

Lyn's hand smoothed Georgy's head shakily. 'He hasn't got a passport,' she replied.

'That can be arranged,' Anatole responded promptly. 'I will see to it.'

Her expression was still troubled. 'I...I may not be al-

lowed to take him out of the country—?' she began, then
stopped.

Anatole frowned. 'You are his aunt—why should he
not travel with you?'

For a second—just a second—he saw in her eyes again
that same emotion he had seen when he had challenged her
as to whether she had adopted Georgy or not.

'You said that the process of adoption is not yet final-
ised,' he said. 'Does that affect whether you can take him
out of the country?'

She swallowed. 'Officially I am still only his foster
carer,' she replied. There was constraint in her voice,
evasiveness in the way her gaze dropped from his. 'I...I
don't know what the rules are about taking foster children abroad...'

'Well, I shall have enquiries made,' said Anatole. 'These
things can be sorted.' He did not want her hiding behind
official rules and regulations. He wanted her to consent
to what he so urgently needed—to bringing Marcos's son
to Greece.

But he would press her no longer. Not for now. Finally
she was listening to him. He had put his request to her—
now he would let her get used to the idea.

He got to his feet, looking down at her. 'It has been,' he
said, and his voice was not unsympathetic now, 'a tumul-
tous day for you—and for myself as well.' His eyes went
to the baby on her lap, who had twisted round to gaze at
him. Once again Anatole felt his heart give a strange convulsion, felt the pulse of emotion go through him.

There was so much of Marcos in the tiny infant!

Almost automatically his eyes slipped to the face of the
young woman holding his infant cousin. He could see the
baby's father in his little face, but what of the tragic mother
who had lost *her* life in giving *him* life? His eyes searched
the aunt's features, looking for an echo of similarity. But

in the clear grey eyes that were ringed with fatigue, in the cheekbones over which the skin was stretched so tightly, in the rigid contours of her jaw, there was no resemblance that he could see.

As his gaze studied her he saw colour suffuse her cheeks and immediately dropped his gaze. He was making her self-conscious, and he did not want to add to her discomfort. Yet as he dropped his gaze he was aware of how the colour in her cheeks gave her a glow, making her less pallid—less plain. More appealing.

She could be something...

The idle thought flicked across his mind and he dismissed it. He was not here to assess whether the aunt of the baby he'd been so desperately seeking possessed those feminine attributes which drew his male eye.

'Forgive me,' he said, his voice contrite. 'I can see my cousin so clearly in his son—I was looking to see what he has inherited from his mother's side.'

He had thought his words might reassure her that he had not been gazing at her with the intention of embarrassing her, but her reaction to his words seemed to have the opposite effect. He saw the colour drain from her face—saw, yet again, that emotion flash briefly in her eyes.

Fear.

He frowned. There was a reason for that reaction—but what was it? He set it aside. For now it was not important. What was important was that he took his leave of her with the lines of communication finally open between them, so that from now on they could discuss what must be discussed—how they were to proceed. How he was to achieve his goal without taking from her the baby nephew she clearly loved so devotedly.

He wanted his last words to her now to be reassuring.

'I will leave you for now,' he said. 'I will visit you again tomorrow—what time would be good for you?'

She swallowed. She had to make some answer. 'I have lectures in the morning, but that's all,' she said hesitantly.

'Good,' he said. 'Then I will come here in the afternoon. We can talk more then. Make more plans.' He paused, looking into her pinched face. 'Plans that we will *both* agree to. Because I know now that you will not give up Georgy—you love him too much. And *you* must surely know that since he cannot be taken from you without your consent, for you are his mother's sister and so the best person to adopt him, that you have nothing to fear from me. Whatever arrangements we make for Georgy's future it will be with your consent and your agreement. You have nothing to fear—nothing at all.'

Surely, he thought, *that* must give her the reassurance that would finally get her to make long-term plans for the infant's upbringing?

But her expression was still withdrawn. Anatole felt determination steal through him. Whatever it took— *whatever!*—he would ensure that his Georgy was reunited with his father's family.

Whatever it took.

He took a breath, looking down at the baby and at the aunt who held him.

'I will see myself out,' he told her. 'Do not disturb yourself.'

Then he was gone.

In the silence that followed his departure the only sound was Georgy contentedly chewing on his plastic keys. Lyn's arms tightened unconsciously around him. She felt weak and shaky and devastated. As if a tsunami had swept over her, drowning her. Her expression was stark.

An overwhelming impulse was coursing through her, imperative in its compulsive force.

The impulse to run. Run far and fast and right away! Run until she had hidden herself from the danger that threatened her—threatened her beloved Georgy! The danger that was in the very person of the tall, dark figure of Anatole Telonidis.

Fear knifed through her.

Anatole threw himself into the back of his car and instructed his driver to head back to the hotel. As the car moved off he got out his mobile. It was time—most definitely time—to phone Timon and tell him what he had discovered.

Who he had discovered.

He had kept everything from Timon until now, loath to raise hopes he could not fulfil. But now—with or without DNA testing—every bone in his body was telling him that he had found Marcos's son.

The son that changed everything.

As his call was put through to his grandfather, and Timon's strained, stricken voice greeted him, Anatole began to speak.

The effect was everything he'd prayed for! Within minutes Timon had become a changed man—a man who had suddenly, miraculously, been given a reason to live. A man who now had only one overriding goal in his life.

'Bring him to me! Bring me Marcos's boy! Do anything and everything you need to get him here!'

Hope had surged in his grandfather's voice. Hope and absolute determination.

'I will,' Anatole replied. 'I will do everything I have to do.'

But as he finished the call his expression changed. Just what 'everything' would need to be he did not fully know. He knew only that, whatever it was, it would all depend on getting Lyn Brandon to agree to it.

As the boy's closest living relative—sister of his mother—his current caregiver and foster mother, with the strongest claim to become Georgy's adoptive mother, it was she who held all the aces.

What would it take to persuade her to let Marcos's son be raised in Greece?

Whatever it was—he had to discover it.

As his mind started to work relentlessly through all the implications and arguments and possibilities a notion started to take shape within his head.

A notion so radical, so drastic, so...*outrageous* that it stopped him in his tracks.

CHAPTER FOUR

'ARE YOU SURE he is not cold?' Anatole frowned as he looked down at the infant sitting up in his buggy.

Lyn shook her head. 'No, honestly, he isn't. He's got lots of layers over him.'

She glanced at the tall figure sitting beside her on the park bench they had walked to. It was a drier day than previously, but spring was still stubbornly far off and she could see why someone used to warmer climes would think it very cold. But it was Anatole Telonidis who had suggested that they take the baby outdoors. Probably, Lyn thought tightly, because a man like him was not used to being in a place as shabby as her flat. Not that this scrappy urban park was a great deal better, but it had a little children's play area where Georgy liked to watch other children playing—as he was doing now.

Even though they had the bench to themselves, it seemed too small to Lyn. She was as punishingly conscious today of Anatole Telonidis's physicality as she had been the day before.

How can he be so devastatingly good-looking?

It was a rhetorical question, and one that every covert glance at him confirmed was unnecessary. It took an effort of will to remind herself brusquely that it was completely irrelevant that she was so punishingly conscious of just how amazing-looking he was.

All that matters is that he wants Georgy to go to Greece...

That was all she had to hold in her mind. Not how strange it felt to be sitting beside him on a chilly park bench, with Georgy's buggy pulled up beside them. A flicker went through her. Others would see a man and a woman in a children's park with a baby in a buggy.

As if they were a family.

A strange little ripple went through her—a little husk of yearning. She was being the best mother she could to Georgy, her beloved sister's son, but however much she tried to substitute for Lindy there was no one to do the same for Georgy's father.

She pushed the thought away. He had *her*, and that was what was important. Essential. Vital. Whatever Anatole wanted to say to her this afternoon, nothing on earth would change that!

'Have you given any more thought to what we spoke of yesterday?' he opened. 'Bringing Georgy out to Greece to meet his grandfather?' He paused minutely. 'I spoke to Timon yesterday.' Anatole's voice changed in a moment, and Lyn could hear the emotion in it. 'I cannot tell you how overjoyed he is to learn of Georgy's existence!'

Lyn's hands twisted in her lap. 'I don't know,' she said. 'I just don't know.' Her eyes went to the man sitting beside her, looking at him with a troubled expression. 'You talk about it being just a visit. But that isn't what you said initially! You said you wanted Georgy to be brought up in Greece! What if you simply don't let Georgy come back here with me? What if you try and keep him in Greece?'

He could hear, once again, the fear spiking in her voice. Resolve formed in him. 'I need you to trust me,' he said.

'How *can* I?' she cried wildly.

Anatole looked at her. Was it going to be like this the whole time? With her doubting everything, distrusting him, fearing him—fighting him? Because he didn't have time for it—and nor did Timon. Timon had undertaken to talk to his oncologist, to find out whether he was too weak to try the strong drugs that he would have to take if he wanted to keep death at bay, even for a little while. For long enough to see his great-grandson and make him his heir, as Anatole so fervently wanted him to do.

He took a deep, scissoring breath that went right down into his lungs. He had promised he would do whatever it took to get Marcos's son out to Greece, to ensure his future was there. But with the baby's aunt resisting him every step of the way, so it seemed, was it not time to take the radical, drastic action that would dispose of all her arguments? All her objections?

It would surely disarm her totally. Yet he was balking at it, he knew. The idea that had sparked in his mind the afternoon before was still alight—but it was so drastic that he still could hardly credit that it had occurred to him at all!

But what else would it take to get her to stop fighting him all the time on what had to happen?

'I understand your fears,' he said now, keeping his voice as reassuring as he could. 'But they are not necessary. I told you—there must be a way to resolve this *impasse* that does not entail conflict.'

Her eyes were wide and troubled. 'I don't see *how*!' she exclaimed. 'You want Georgy to be brought up in Greece, with his father's family. I want to keep him here with me. How can those two possibly be resolved?'

Anatole chose his words with care. 'What if you came with Georgy?' he asked.

She stared at him blankly. 'Brought him out to visit your grandfather?'

He gave a quick shake of his head. 'Not just to visit—to live.'

'To *live* in Greece?' she echoed, as if she had not heard properly. 'Georgy and me?'

'Why not?' Anatole's eyes were studying her reaction.

'But I'm British!' she replied blankly, because right now it was the only thing that occurred to her.

The corner of his mouth curved, and irrelevantly Lyn thought how it lightened his expression—and sent a pulse of blood around her veins. Then he was replying.

'Many British people live very happily in Greece,' he said dryly. 'They find the climate a great deal warmer!' he said pointedly, glancing around at the bleak, wintry landscape.

'But I haven't got any accountancy qualifications yet, and even when I do I probably wouldn't be able to practise out there. And besides, I don't speak any Greek! How could I make a living?'

Anatole's eyebrows rose. Had she *really* just asked that question?

'It goes without saying,' he said, and his voice was even drier, 'that there would be no necessity for you to do so.'

His reply was a flash of her grey eyes that gave animation to her thin face.

'I'm *not* living on charity!' she objected.

Anatole shook his head. 'It would not be a question of charity!' he retorted. His tone of voice changed. 'Timon would insist that you have an allowance.'

Her mouth pressed together. 'So I'd be Georgy's paid nursemaid? Is that what you're saying?'

'*No!*' She was taking this entirely the wrong way, he could see. He tried to recover. 'How could you be a nurse-maid when you are going to be Georgy's adoptive mother?'

He had thought his words would be reassuring to her, yet for a second there was again that flash of fearful emotion he had seen before in her eyes. His gaze narrowed infinitesimally. 'Tell me,' he heard himself saying, 'is there some problem with your application to adopt Georgy?'

It was a shot fired with a calculated aim to expose any

weaknesses in her claim. Weaknesses, he knew with grim resolve, he would have to exploit if she reverted to being as obdurate and uncooperative as she had been yesterday. But surely that would not be so—not now that they had finally reached the stage where they could at least discuss Georgy's future without her flying into an emotional storm!

He watched her face, saw her expression close. His shot had hit home, he could see.

'What is it?' he asked bluntly.

Lyn's hands twisted in her lap. Unease and fear writhed in her. But she had to reply—that much was obvious.

'From the moment Lindy died,' she said, her voice low and strained, 'the authorities wanted Georgy taken into care and put up for adoption. Adoption not by me but by a childless couple. There are so many desperate for a baby!'

A cold spear went through Anatole. It was just as he had feared the moment Lyn Brandon had said that she was not Georgy's birth mother!

'Even now,' she said tightly, 'if I dropped my application they would hand him over straight away to a married couple!'

'But you are his maternal aunt. That surely gives you a priority claim to him!'

The fear darted in her eyes again. 'They say I'm too young, that I'm a student still, that I'd be a single mother—' Her voice broke.

For a moment Anatole was silent.

'But I'm not giving in!' Lyn's voice was vehement now. 'I'll *never* give in—no matter what they say or how much they drag their heels! I'll never give up Georgy! *Never!*'

Her hands spasmed in her lap, anguish knifing inside her. Then suddenly her hands were being covered by a large, warm, strong hand, stilling their convulsion.

'There is a way.' Anatole heard himself speaking but

did not quite believe he was doing so. 'There is a way that could solve the entire dilemma.'

Lyn's eyes flew to his. He felt their impact—read the fear in them.

'You say that two of the arguments being used against your adopting Georgy are that you are still a student—unwaged and unmarried,' he said. Part of his brain was still wondering whether he would truly say what he was about to hear himself saying. 'What if neither of those things were true any more? What if you became a stay-at-home mother who could devote her days to Georgy—who had a husband to provide for you both and be the father figure that Georgy needs?'

She was looking blank. Totally blank.

'I don't understand,' she said.

Anatole's hand pressed hers. 'What if,' he said, 'that husband—that father figure—were me?'

For a timeless moment she simply stared at him with huge, blank eyes. Then, with a jolt, she moved away, pulling her hands free from his. They felt cold without his covering clasp, but that didn't matter. All that mattered was that she say what was searing through her head.

'That's insane!'

Anatole gave a quick shake of his head. He had expected that reaction. It was, after all, exactly the reaction he'd had himself when the notion had first inserted itself into his brain yesterday, as he sought for ways to sort out the infernally complicated situation he was in.

'Not insane—logical.' He held up a hand. 'Listen to me—hear me out.' He took a breath, his eyes going absently to Georgy, who was still, he was glad to see, totally absorbed with chewing on his beloved set of keys while avidly watching the toddlers tottering about on the park's play equipment.

'This is what I propose,' he said, turning his gaze back to Lyn.

She had gone white as a sheet, with the same stark expression in her face he had seen yesterday. It did not flatter her, he found himself thinking. But he brushed that aside. Her looks were not important right now. What was important was getting her to see the world his way—as fast as he possibly could.

'If we were to marry, it would solve all our problems in one stroke. For the authorities here it would dispose of their objection to you being a single mother, as yet unable to support a child financially. Moreover, in addition to your being Georgy's maternal aunt, the fact that you would be marrying someone who's the closest thing to Georgy's uncle as can be has to be compelling! And finally—' his voice was dry now '—there would be absolutely no question about my ability to support a family financially!'

She was still staring at him as if he were mad. 'But you're a complete stranger! I only met you yesterday!'

And you are about as far removed from anyone I am likely to marry as it is possible to be!

That was the consciousness that was burning in her most fiercely, making her feel hot and cold at the same time, overriding all that he had been saying about the logic behind his insane idea!

Anatole gave a shrug. 'All married couples were strangers once,' he pointed out. There was still a sense of disbelief within him. Was he *really* saying this to the girl sitting beside him? Seriously talking about *marrying* her?

Yet the logic was irrefutable! It was *the* most effective way of achieving what had to be achieved—getting Marcos's son out to Greece, to be raised as Timon's heir.

'Think about it,' he urged. 'I'll give you time—obviously! —but I beg you to give it serious consideration.'

As he looked at her he thought, privately, that right now

she couldn't give serious consideration to anything short of a tornado heading for her—she was still staring at him totally blankly.

'I can't *possibly* marry you! It's…it's just the most absurd thing I've ever heard!' Her voice was high-pitched with shock.

'It isn't absurd—' he began.

'Yes, it is! It's completely absurd—and…and…'

She couldn't go on, was bereft of speech, and he took ruthless advantage of her floundering.

'The purpose of our marriage would be solely to ensure Georgy's future,' he said. 'Once that has been achieved, then…' he took a breath, never taking his eyes from her '…then there will be no need for it to exist.'

She blinked. 'I don't understand.'

'This is what I envisage,' Anatole explained. 'Marriage between us will surely secure Georgy's adoption—we are the closest living relatives he has—but once he has been adopted then there will be no compelling reason why we have to stay married. We can get divorced.' His expression changed. 'Provided Georgy continues to be raised in Greece.'

'Why is that so important?' she asked.

'Timon will insist,' he answered. He paused a moment. 'Timon will make Georgy his heir. He will inherit the Petranakos Corporation when Timon dies—just as Marcos would have done, had he lived.'

Lyn frowned. 'But *you* are his grandson too,' she said. 'Why won't you inherit?'

Anatole gave a quick negating shake of his head. 'I am Timon's *daughter's* son—I am not a Petranakos. I have my own inheritance from my late father and I do *not*,' he emphasised, 'seek Georgy's. What I *do* seek—' he took a scissoring breath '—are the powers required to run Petranakos until Georgy's majority.' His eyes rested on Lyn.

'I do not need to tell you how very grave the economic situation is in Greece at the moment. Unemployment is rife and causing considerable distress. The situation at Petranakos is…difficult. And it has become more so since Timon's illness. Worse, when Marcos was killed Timon decided to make a distant Petranakos cousin his heir—a man who, quite frankly, couldn't run a bath, let alone a multi-million-euro business in a highly precarious economy! If he inherits,' Anatole said flatly, 'he'll run it in to the ground and thousands will lose their jobs! I will *not* stand by and watch that happen!'

He took another breath and kept his eyes on Lyn, willing her to understand what was driving him. 'I know exactly what I need to do to get it on track again and safeguard all the jobs it provides. But for that to happen Timon will insist that Georgy grows up in Greece.'

She heard the steel in his voice, the determination. Yet that did not change her reaction to what had to be the most absurd, insane suggestion she'd ever heard in her life! Even if he was wishing they could divorce later…

She opened her mouth to say so, but he was still speaking.

'You can see just why a marriage between us makes sense! Not only does it keep the adoption authorities happy, but it keeps Timon happy too! He will know that Marcos's son will be raised in Greece, under my guardianship, once his days are gone.'

And that, Anatole knew, would be exactly what Timon would want. He would expect Anatole to take care of Marcos's son, raise him as his own.

That is what I want, too!

The realisation hit him as his eyes went once again to the diminutive figure in the buggy. Emotion welled through Anatole. Of *course* he would look after Marcos's son—there was no question that he would not! He had known of his existence such a short time, known the tiny bundle for even less, but already that tiny bundle had seized upon his heart. He would never abandon him—*never*. That was an indelible certainty now.

Whatever it took to make certain of it!

Whatever...

'It's still impossible! Completely impossible!'

Her voice, still high-pitched and strained, made him twist his head back round to her. She saw his expression change. Something about it sent a shaft of fear spearing through her.

He spoke quietly, but there was a quality to that quietness that made her tense—something about the way his veiled eyes were resting on her. 'Please understand that if we cannot agree on this, then...' he paused a moment, then said what he knew he must say to her, to make it clear that he was set on this course. 'Then I will put in an application to adopt Georgy myself, as his closest, most suitable relative on his father's side.'

He had said it. And it had on her the impact he'd known it must. She paled again, her skin taut and white over her cheekbones.

He pressed on relentlessly. 'Do you really want to take the risk that my claim to Georgy may supersede yours, despite my only being his second cousin, not his mother's sister, as you are?'

She seemed to shrink away from him, and the flash of fear in her eyes was the strongest yet. He could see her face working, her hands clenching and unclenching in her lap.

He covered them again with his own. Set his gaze on her. 'It doesn't have to be like that—truly it does not. I do not want confrontation or conflict. I want you to trust me—trust me that what I am suggesting, that we solve this situation by agreeing to marry, is the best way forward.'

She was still shrinking away from him, her expression still fearful.

'I need you to trust me,' he said again.

She could feel his gaze pouring into her, willing her to accept what he was saying. But how could she? How could she possibly accept it?

He'll try and adopt Georgy himself! He'll use the pots of money he's got—that Georgy's great-grandfather's got—and throw it at lawyers and judges and just go on and on and on...

And it was not just his money that would give him the power to take Georgy from her...

Fear coursed through her again—so familiar—so terrifying.

She gave a little cry, jumping to her feet, pulling free of the clasp that was so warm and strong on her hand.

'I don't want this! I don't want any of this! I just want to go back to the way it was!'

He got to his feet too. A sigh escaped him. He understood her reaction.

'I, too, wish we could go back,' he said quietly, but now the quietness was different. It was threaded with sombre emotion. 'I wish I could go back to before Timon was diagnosed with terminal cancer, to before he gave that lethal car to Marcos, to before Marcos smashed himself to pieces in it. But I can't go back. And neither can you. All we *can* do...' his eyes sought to convey the ineluctable truth '...is go forward as best we can.'

His eyes went to Georgy. Softened. Then back to Lyn, standing there trembling in every line of her body.

'And the best that we want is for Georgy.'

Right on cue Marcos's baby son seemed to hear himself addressed and turned his head enquiringly. Anatole went over and hunkered down to pay him attention. Lyn stood, looking down at them both. Emotion was churning in her over and over, like a washing machine inside her.

Anatole glanced up at her. He could see how over-wrought she was. It was time to lighten the atmosphere.

'Come,' he said, holding out a hand towards her. 'We have had enough heavy stuff for the moment. Let's take a break from it. Tell me,' he asked, glancing towards the swings and slides, 'can Georgy go on any of those yet?'

She nodded, swallowing. 'He likes the slide, but you have to hold him—don't let him go!' she said.

'Great,' said Anatole.

He unfastened the safety belt of the buggy and drew Georgy out. Georgy gave a crow of excitement. Lyn stood watching them interact—Anatole talking to him in what she realised must be Greek. A little pang went through her. Georgy was as much Greek as he was English. Could she truly deny him all that his father's family could offer him?

He will be the heir to a fortune.

She might not care, but wouldn't Georgy want that inheritance when he grew up? Wouldn't he want to be part of his Greek heritage as well?

Yet what Anatole Telonidis had just proposed was absurd—no one could say otherwise, no one at all!

A chill crept through her. Except if she did *not* agree to that absurdity then he had made it very clear—ruthlessly clear—that he would seek to adopt Georgy himself.

Fear knifed her. *I can't lose Georgy—I can't!*

The cry—so familiar, so desperate—sounded in her head, her heart.

She watched Anatole carry Georgy over to the slide, hold him on the slippery surface halfway up and then whoosh him down to the end, to Georgy's patent delight. He repeated the whole process over and over again, and she heard his words resonate in her head. She could not go back to the way it had been when it was just Georgy and her. That was over now—*over*. All she could do was go forward. Forward into a future that seemed frighteningly uncertain. Full of risks of losing Georgy for ever.

I have to do whatever I can to prevent that—whatever I can to safeguard him, keep him with me. I have to do whatever it takes.

And if that meant taking the most insane, most absurd decision of her life then she would have to do it...

'If...' Lyn began slowly. 'If we...go ahead...with what you said...then...' She tried to make herself stop talking so hesitantly, but couldn't. 'How long do you think—um—before we could—well—divorce?'

'It depends,' said Anatole. He'd lifted Georgy off the slide and returned to sit next to Lyn, keeping hold of Georgy. It felt good to have the weight of his solid little body perched on his knees. He'd presented Georgy with his favourite plastic keys, and the little hands shot them straight to his mouth to start chewing on them enthusiastically.

He felt his heart clutch, thinking of the tragedy that had befallen his wayward, headstrong young cousin, who had not deserved to die so young, so brutally. Leaving his helpless child behind.

But his son has me now—me to care for him—to guard his interests, ensure his future.

'On what?'

Lyn's thin voice dispersed his memory, his vehement thoughts. He took a breath, focusing on what she'd said, this woman he'd met only the day before whom he was now telling he wanted to marry.

And then divorce again as soon as possible.

'Well, I guess whatever is the minimum time needed, really. I'm not sure what the law is—or if it's different in Greece from here. Obviously the adoption has to go through first, since that's the whole reason for getting married.'

Lyn frowned. 'I think there are laws about not getting married…well, *artificially*. You know—the law says it has to be a genuine marriage.' She swallowed uneasily.

Anatole did not seem fazed. 'Well, it will be, won't it? We will genuinely get married in order to provide security for our orphaned relative. I don't see any problem with that.'

The problem, thought Lyn wildly, was in the very idea of her marrying Anatole Telonidis at all! She swallowed again. 'When…when would it actually happen? The—um—wedding?'

'Ah…' he answered. 'Well, again, I believe there are legal timescales—and, again, I don't know what the law is here on how soon a couple can marry.' His eyes moved to her and held hers. 'The thing is, we will need to marry in Greece. Timon,' he said, 'is not well enough to travel.'

'Greece…' echoed Lyn, her voice hollow.

Anatole's mouth quirked, and Lyn felt that little pulse go through her, as it had when she had first seen humour lighten his face.

'You speak of my country as though it were the far side of the moon,' he said wryly.

'I—I've never been there,' she answered.

'Then you are in for a pleasant surprise. My grandfather lives outside Athens, within commuting distance, on the coast. His villa is at the shoreline, with its own beach, where Marcos and I used to play as children when we visited our grandfather. What I suggest is that you and I make our base not in the main villa—which is massive and very old-fashioned—but in the beach house, which is much more manageable and also goes straight out onto the sand beyond the terrace. It will be ideal for Georgy.'

His voice had warmed and Lyn tried to sound appreciative. 'That would be nice...' she said.

Nice—the word echoed in Anatole's head. Yes, Timon's palatial villa with its luxuriously appointed beach house set in extensive private gardens would indeed be 'nice' for someone whose current accommodation was a cramped, dingy furnished flat in a hideous sixties concrete block...

'Does that reassure you?' he asked.

No! she wanted to shout. *No. Absolutely nothing about this insane idea reassures me!*

But what was the point of saying that? Of course the idea was insane and absurd and outrageous—but Anatole Telonidis was taking it seriously. Talking about it as if it were really going to happen.

Am I really going to go through with this? Go through with marriage to a man I never knew existed forty-eight hours ago?

A man she was a million miles removed from—a man who lived in the distant stratosphere of the rich, while she was an impecunious student struggling along the breadline.

It wasn't as if she were like Lindy, she thought bitterly. Lindy with her lovely blonde hair, her blue eyes and curvaceous figure. No wonder she'd drawn the philandering eye of Marcos Petranakos when she'd lived in London. If Lyn had possessed Lindy's looks she wouldn't feel so abysmally awkward, sitting here talking about something as intimate as marriage to a man like Anatole Telonidis.

But it won't be 'intimate' will it? she castigated herself roundly. *If it's absurd and insane to think of marrying him, it's beyond either to think of anything at all beyond the merest formality. It will be a marriage in name only, solely and simply for the purpose of safeguarding Georgy.*

She and Anatole would be presenting a united front to convince the adoption authorities that they were the best possible parents for him. And if they didn't present a united front…if Anatole applied for Georgy entirely on his own…

Fear stabbed at her. If that happened then he would inevitably discover what she must not let him find out…

Must not!

'Lyn?'

His deep, accented voice interrupted her troubled emotions. She jerked her head up and felt the impact of his gaze, felt the flurry in her veins that came as his eyes rested on her, his look enquiring.

'Are we agreed?' he asked. 'Have I convinced you that this is the very best possible step for us to take?'

She bit her lip. She wanted time—time to think, to focus! But how would that help? The longer she delayed, prevaricated, the more likely it was that Anatole Telonidis would get impatient and set his lawyers to the task of making a formal application to adopt Georgy himself.

She took a breath, ragged and uneven. 'OK,' she said. 'OK, I'll do it.'

CHAPTER FIVE

LYN GAZED AROUND her. The room Anatole Telonidis had ushered her into, Georgy clutched in her arms, was huge. Pale pristine carpet stretched in front of her, upon which was set cream-upholstered sofas and armchairs. Vast picture windows took up one entire wall, looking out over one of London's West End parks. It couldn't have been more different from her cramped little flat. Yet it was where she was going to stay until she went to Athens.

To marry Anatole Telonidis.

She felt the familiar eddy of shock go through her as she faced up to what she had agreed to. But it was too late now—the decision had been made. She had quit her college course, moved out of her flat, travelled down to London with Anatole in his chauffeur-driven car, and her personal belongings had been conveyed by carrier.

He had taken charge of everything, sweeping her along with him so that she hardly knew what was happening any more—except that it was an overturning of everything familiar. Now he turned to look at her as she stared at the luxury apartment he'd rented.

'Come and choose which bedroom you want for you and Georgy,' he said, and led the way back out in to the spacious hallway, off which several bedrooms opened. She knew which one she would choose—whichever was

furthest away from the master bedroom, where Anatole
would be.

A flush went through her. How on earth was she to live
in such close quarters with a man who was a complete
stranger to her? And, worse than that, a man who was,
when it came to physical attributes, a million miles away
from her nondescript appearance.

What on earth does that matter? she robustly admonished herself as she inspected the bedrooms. As she kept
reminding herself, hoping to be reassured, theirs was to be
a marriage in name only, solely for the purpose of adopting Georgy, placating the authorities.

Anatole was speaking again, and she made herself listen.

'There is a gym and a swimming pool for residents
in the basement. The park is accessible directly from the
apartment block, which will be convenient for taking
Georgy out. The apartment is fully serviced, so all meals
can be delivered as in a hotel. Plus, of course, groceries
and anything else you want can be delivered too. Obviously
there's a maid service, so you won't have any housework
to do.' He took a breath and then went on. 'Order whatever you want for Georgy by way of equipment, toys and
clothes. Everything can be taken out to Greece when we
go. A credit card will be delivered to you shortly, and I
am arranging for a new bank account for you, into which
I will pay sufficient funds for you to draw on.'

He paused, and looked at her. She seemed to be taking
it in, but it was hard to tell. She had scarcely opened her
mouth. Well, she was still in a state of shock, he conceded.
Her life had been turned upside down, and she was trying
to come to terms with it. Just as he was....

For a treacherous moment he heard his inner voice re-
monstrating with him, telling him that it was insane to
do what he was doing, but he silenced it. There was no

backing out now. Not for him—or her. They just had to get on with it.

He made his voice soften. 'It's strange for you, I know,' he said, taking a step towards her. 'But you will get used to things soon enough. I am sorry I have to leave you straight away, but it is necessary. I have to see my grandfather and talk to his doctors about what treatment he might be able to have. I have to tell him our plans and urge him to make Georgy his heir, put me in charge of the Petranakos Corporation as soon as possible. Then I have to attend to some urgent business affairs of my own, which have been neglected since I flew to England. In the meantime,' he finished, 'my lawyers are liaising with your social services on an application for Georgy's passport and permission to take him out of the country, as well as everything to do with our forthcoming marriage and how it can accelerate the adoption process. I'll only be in Athens a couple of days. Then I will come right back here.'

He smiled at her in a way he hoped was reassuring. 'I'm sure that you will be feeling more settled by then. You have my personal mobile number, so of course do phone whenever you want if there is anything that worries you.'

A little burst of hysteria bubbled through Lyn. *You mean like anything other than the fact I'm actually going to go ahead and marry you?*

But there was no point saying that. No point doing anything other than nod and clutch Georgy more tightly to her.

'Good,' said Anatole briskly, and lifted his hand to take Georgy's outstretched fingers. This tiny bundle of humanity was what was bringing him and this alien female together. His expression softened. He murmured some infantile nonsense to the baby in Greek, then shifted his gaze to the woman holding him.

'It will be all right,' he said. 'Trust me—please.'

He flickered a brief smile at her, and a warmer one at

Georgy, who was trying to get at his tie again. 'Uh-uh,' he said reprovingly, and chucked him under the chin. 'Be good, young man, and look after your aunt for me,' he instructed.

Georgy gazed at him wide-eyed. Lyn gave an awkward smile.

'See you at the weekend,' said Anatole, and headed for the door.

Behind him, Lyn slowly sank down on to one of the pristine sofas.

She felt completely numb.

Over the next two days she gradually started to feel less numb—less in shock. And gradually, too, she became used to her new surroundings. Although she was worried Georgy might make a mess of the pristine decor, she could not help but find the luxury, warmth and comfort of the apartment very easy to appreciate after the privations of her dingy flat. The milder air of the capital drew her out to the park, with Georgy enthroned in a brand-new, top-of-the-range buggy delivered from a top London store.

She was just returning from such an outing on her third day in the apartment, wheeling Georgy into the spacious hallway, when she realised she was not alone.

Anatole strolled out of the living room.

Immediately Georgy crowed with delight and recognition, holding out his chubby arms. Lyn's senses reeled as she took in Anatole's tall, elegant figure and dark good-looks. He was wearing a suit but had discarded the jacket, loosened his shirt collar and cuffs. The effect of the slight informality of his appearance made her stomach tighten. He looked lean and powerful and devastatingly masculine.

He glanced a smile of greeting at her, and hunkered down to extract Georgy. Hefting him out, he held him up and swung him high in both hands. He greeted him in Greek, then did likewise, in English, to Lyn.

'Hi,' she murmured awkwardly, and busied herself folding up the buggy and putting it away in the hall cupboard.

She let Anatole keep Georgy and, taking off her baggy jacket and hanging it up beside the buggy, followed them into the living room. It was no longer quite as pristine as it had once been. One sofa had been covered by a fleecy throw—more to protect its pale covers than to protect Georgy—on the thick carpet another throw was spread out, arrayed with a good selection of Georgy's toys.

She watched Anatole carefully lower the baby down on to the floor, where Georgy gleefully seized upon one of his soft toys.

Anatole stood back, watching him. His mood was resolute. The time he'd spent in Greece had seen to that. His grandfather was a changed man, summoning all his doctors and demanding the very latest drugs, determined to live now for as long as he could. Determined, too, to see his great-grandson restored to his family. Even if it required Anatole to resort to this drastic strategy to make that happen.

Timon had seemed to take a moment or two to absorb Anatole's announcement, his face blanking as if in shock, but then he had simply waved an impatient hand. 'If it keeps all the damn officials happy and speeds everything up, it's worth it,' Timon had said. Then he'd cast a sly look at his grandson. 'I take it she's got other charms than just being the boy's aunt?'

Anatole's eyes rested on the figure stiffly sitting herself down on sofa, busying herself playing with Georgy. No, the charms that Timon had been implying she might have were conspicuously absent. She still looked just as she had when he'd first set eyes on her, with her dark hair pulled back apart from some straggly bits pushed behind her ears, no make-up, and wearing a shapeless jumper and jeans that bagged at the knees. Yet as he studied her, watched her playing with Georgy, his eyes went to her face and his blighting assessment wavered.

If he dragged his gaze away from her dire hair and worse clothes he could see that her pale skin was clear and unblemished, and her grey eyes were well set beneath defined brows, sparkling now with animation as she laughed with Georgy. The shape of her face was oval, he noted, with a delicate bone structure, and there was something about the line of her mouth that held his glance...

He watched her a moment longer, resolve forming within him. She could not possibly turn up in Greece as his fiancée looking the way she did now, so badly dressed and unkempt.

Well, that could be sorted, but right now he was hungry. He hadn't eaten on the flight, and it was lunchtime. First he needed a shower, a change of clothes and to check his e-mails, and then he would take Lyn and Georgy for lunch.

And after lunch, he resolved, he would take them shopping. Toys for Georgy—new clothes for Lyn.

Everyone would be happy. Including him.

An hour later they were ready to set off. Lyn was not enthusiastic about the expedition, Anatole could tell, but she had acquiesced docilely enough. She'd changed her clothes, though the brown skirt and pale cream blouse were not a great improvement, to his mind. The skirt was overlong and the blouse too baggy. But that didn't matter—after lunch she would be getting a whole new wardrobe.

Over lunch, his sense of resolve strengthened. He would start getting to know her. There must be no awkwardness between them. Georgy united them, and that meant they could not remain strangers. Little by little he had to win her over, get her to relax in his company.

Get her to trust him.

But she was clearly feeling awkward and totally unrelaxed—that much was obvious to him as they made their way into the restaurant he'd selected. A few diners cast disapproving glances at Georgy in his carrier as they took their seats, but since he was looking both angelic and deeply slumberous no one said anything.

Lyn sat down on the plush banquette, feeling acutely uncomfortable. Her dull, chainstore clothes were completely out of place in such an expensive locale, but there was nothing she could do about it. Since she didn't look like the kind of woman a man like Anatole Telonidis would socialise with, there was no point making an idiot of herself by trying to and failing.

Anatole took charge, ordering drinks and food. Lyn stared around her uneasily, unused to such expensive surroundings. She jumped as the wine waiter reappeared and opened a bottle of champagne with a soft pop.

The effervescent liquid was poured out, and as the waiter departed with a bow Anatole lifted his glass. 'Let us drink to Georgy's future,' he said.

He was trying to be encouraging, she could see. Gingerly, Lyn raised her glass and took a nervous sip. It tasted very dry, and the bubbles burst on her tongue with a slightly acerbic texture. She set the glass down.

'You don't care for it?' Anatole's voice sounded surprised. It was an excellent vintage.

'Sorry, the only fizzy wine I've ever had before has been very sweet,' Lyn apologised.

'This is not "fizzy wine",' said Anatole severely. 'This is champagne.'

Lyn flushed. 'I'm sorry,' she mumbled again.

'There is absolutely no need for apology,' he said promptly.

He started on an explanation of what constituted champagne, and Lyn found herself listening attentively. It wasn't a subject that had ever crossed her path before. As she listened she took some more little sips of the crisp, sparkling liquid, and as she sipped she started to feel that taut wire of tension running down her spine lessening almost imperceptibly.

Their first course arrived—little *rondelles* of salmon pâté lightened with a lemon *jus*—and Lyn found them delicious.

From champagne, Anatole broadened out into discussing wine in general. It seemed a pretty safe topic, in the circumstances.

'Even here in the UK you are starting to produce some very acceptable white wines,' he commented.

'It was the Romans, I think, who first planted vines in Britain,' Lyn ventured. She had to make some kind of effort with conversation. She owed it to Anatole to make this intensely awkward meal less awkward. 'The climate was warmer then—the Roman Warm Period that ended around 400 AD.'

Anatole's expression registered surprise. 'That's very detailed historical knowledge for someone studying accountancy,' he said.

'I really wanted to study history,' Lyn explained diffidently. 'But it's not the best subject for post-graduate employment—especially not since I already count as a mature student, being in my mid-twenties now. Accountancy's far more likely to earn me a good enough living to raise Georgy—' She broke off, conscious that Georgy's financial future was very different now.

'Well, Greece has more history than anywhere else in Europe,' Anatole said. 'And a great deal of it is in Athens.' He spoke lightly, steering the conversation towards classical Greek history. The champagne, he could tell, was starting to help her relax, become more talkative.

'How did you find the service dining in the apartment while I was in Greece?' he enquired as they ate.

She looked up. 'Oh, I haven't used it. It's bound to be very expensive. I've found a small grocery store locally, down a side street, so I've been cooking for myself and Georgy.'

'You really do not have to stint yourself when it comes to the facilities of the apartment,' Anatole said dryly. 'Tell me, have you taken Georgy swimming in the pool?'

She shook her head. 'Not yet,' she said.

'We shall buy him some pool toys this afternoon,' Anatole said. 'All sorts of toys,' he added expansively while he was at it.

Lyn brightened. 'Oh, yes, please—that would be wonderful! He really needs some that are more advanced for the next stage of his development.' She smiled. 'He's very nearly ready to crawl, and when that happens he's going to take off like a rocket!'

The conversation moved on to Georgy, the subject of their mutual interest and the reason for their marriage. As if hearing his name mentioned, Georgy decided to surface from his slumber. Enlivened by his sleep, he made it clear he wanted out of his carrier and into Lyn's arms. Settling him on her lap, she busied herself feeding him from a pot of baby yoghurt she'd thought to bring with her in between taking sips of coffee to finish her meal.

Then, replete and ready for the off, they left—Georgy borne happily aloft as they exited the restaurant, his little arms waving cheerily at what he fondly took to be his admiring fellow diners. Settled into the waiting chauffeured car, they set off for the shops.

The department store they went to was, Lyn resigned herself to accept, one of London's most expensive and luxurious. Since the buggy and baby carrier had been delivered from there, she was not surprised that Anatole seemed to regard it as the obvious place to shop. Certainly the toy department was lavish beyond anything—and so, she very shortly realised, was Anatole's determination to purchase a substantial amount from the infant section of it, much of it way too advanced for Georgy.

'He can't possibly do a fifty-piece jigsaw!' Lyn exclaimed. 'He needs toys that say nine to twelve months—that's all.'

Anatole frowned. 'He is a very intelligent child,' he observed.

'Nine to twelve months,' Lyn repeated firmly. 'Look—that thing there is ideal!'

She pointed to a large moulded plastic construction, a colourful house and farmyard, with big doors and windows and a roof that all came to bits and slotted together again. Around the perimeter was a railway track with a train and truck, containing people and animals for the house and farmyard. A large, baby-operable lever set the train whizzing around the house, ringing a bell as it did so. Lyn demonstrated its mode of operation on the display model and instantly caught Georgy's attention.

Anatole promptly lifted down a boxed unit. 'What else?' he said, looking around him.

Lyn found herself guiding him through the selection process. It felt awkward, initially, having to be so proactive, but she soon realised that she knew a lot more about what was suitable than Anatole did. He deferred to her without demur, and gradually she found that it was getting easier to be in his company like this. It was even, she realised, enjoyable. And Georgy took such enthusiastic interest in this Aladdin's cave of toys, as well as clearly relishing the presence of lots of other babies and infants, that she found her eyes meeting Anatole's as they shared Georgy's enjoyment.

But that sense of communication ended abruptly as they left the toy department.

'While we are here, Lyn, I would like to look in at the women's fashion floor,' Anatole said.

She halted. 'What for?'

He looked down at her face. She had tensed immediately and her expression was wary. Carefully, he sought the right way to say what he wanted.

'I appreciate that your circumstances till now have been straitened financially,' he began, keeping his tone neutral, 'and of course you have had a great deal to cope with, looking after Georgy while pursuing your studies. I can understand those have been your priorities. Now, however, things are different.' He took a breath. 'New clothes for your new life—'

'I don't need any new clothes!'

'Lyn, you need a whole new wardrobe,' he said.

'No, I don't! It's fine as it is! *Really!*'

He could hear the intensity in her voice and found himself wondering at it. Didn't she want something better to wear than what she had to put up with?

'Please,' she went on, with the same intensity in her voice, 'I don't want you spending money on me!'

His mouth pressed tightly. 'Lyn, you are going to be my wife—of *course* I will spend money on you! I have quite a lot to spend,' he reminded her. 'I don't mean to sound extravagant, and I know you have had to be very careful with money—I have a great deal of respect for you for that—but now things are different.' He paused. 'Don't you *want* to have a new wardrobe? I thought new clothes were something all women wanted!' He put a note of humour into his voice, as if to lighten the tension.

It didn't work. She was staring at him, and her expression remained fraught. Did he really think lashing out on expensive clothes would actually do anything for her? Of course it wouldn't! She would just feel awkward and embarrassed and horrible!

'I'm fine with what I've got,' she managed to get out.

Dark flashes glinted in Anatole's eyes, but he veiled them. She might be fine with what she had, but he was not—it was absurd for her to be dressed the way she was. But he took a silent breath. For now he would not pressure her.

'OK,' he said, holding up his hand. 'If that's truly what you prefer.'

'It is,' she said gratefully. Then, casting about to change the subject, she said hurriedly, 'But what I *do* need, however, is some more clothes for Georgy—he's growing rapidly.' She hesitated. 'I'm sure the baby clothes here will be very expensive—I can get them much cheaper elsewhere, so—'

'Here is fine, Lyn,' Anatole interrupted her firmly, and set off towards babywear, next to the toy department.

Lyn hurried after him, pushing the buggy. She felt weak at the narrow escape she'd had. It would have been unendurable to go down to the fashion department and have some snooty vendeuse look pityingly at her while she tried on designer fashions to try and conceal her nondescript looks. She would have writhed with embarrassment and self-consciousness!

Instead, all she had to do now was try not to blanch when she looked at the price tags on the baby clothes that Anatole was holding up for her inspection. If he was going to spend his money at least it would be on Georgy, not her, so she made little objection. Nor did she object when, purchases made, Anatole had them taken down to his chauffeured car. Then, turning to Lyn, he suggested they find the store's tea lounge.

As she sat herself down on a soft banquette, tea ordered

from the waitress and Anatole amusing Georgy with one of his smaller new toys, she found herself observing them.

Emotion moved within her. He was so good with Georgy—naturally attentive and responsive, clearly enjoying interacting with him—and Georgy, too, was clearly enjoying being with Anatole.

That's why I'm doing this, she reminded herself fiercely. *For Georgy's sake!*

Yet even as she said the words in her head she knew, somewhere deep inside her, a little ache had started up, as she gazed at the man holding her beloved Georgy. What if there were no Georgy and Anatole Telonidis, with his amazing looks, his dark, expressive eyes, his lean strength and honed physique, were going to marry her not because of an orphaned baby but for herself alone?

Even as the thought formed she squashed it flat.

Without Georgy Anatole Telonidis would never even have looked her way...

That was what she had to remember. Only that—however crushing the knowledge.

With a silent little sigh, she got on with drinking her tea.

CHAPTER SIX

OVER THE WEEKEND she slowly got used to Anatole being in such close quarters with her. She took Georgy out into the park a lot, now the weather was more clement, leaving Anatole to work, as he told her he must, for he had a lot to catch up with. The apartment had an office, and Anatole disappeared in there, focusing on his laptop and phone. The plan was, he told her, to go to Athens as soon as Georgy had his passport issued and was cleared to leave the country with his foster carer.

'Hopefully,' Anatole had said over dinner that first night, 'my legal team will be able to put sufficient pressure on the authorities to expedite matters. As for Timon—he's now starting treatment, and we must hope that it takes effect. He'll stay in hospital for the time being, since these drugs have side effects he may find it difficult to tolerate and he is an old man in his eighties. But soon—within a few weeks, I very much hope—he will be discharged and able to come home again. And once he's home...' he smiled at Lyn '...we can get on with getting married.'

He paused, looking at her. Her expression was tense again.

'Lyn,' he said, with deliberate lightness, 'this is your *wedding* we're planning—'

'It's not a real one,' she said, and then wished she hadn't. She hadn't wanted to imply that she wanted a *real* wedding to Anatole Telondis! It would be excruciatingly embarrassing if he thought that!

But all he said was, 'Well, it's going to be a happy occasion, anyway. It will secure Georgy's future, and that is what we want.' He took a breath, his expression changing somewhat. 'That said, it can't be a large wedding, as I'm sure you'll understand. That would be…inappropriate, given how recently Marcos died.'

'Of course,' Lyn said immediately, and knew she was grateful not to have to face some huge society bash. That would be as embarrassing as Anatole thinking she wanted her marriage to him to be a real one.

This is all about Georgy—only about Georgy! That's all I have to remember!

Even so, until they were able to divorce she would have to go through with being in such close quarters with Anatole as she was now. It was becoming easier, she'd discovered gratefully. He was obviously making a real effort to try and get her to feel more comfortable, to draw her out and get to know her. It felt awkward for her, but she did her best to co-operate.

'Tell me,' he went on now, moving on from the subject of their wedding, 'why did you not go to college straight after school?'

'Well, it wasn't really possible,' Lyn answered. 'Lindy was only fourteen, and I couldn't leave her.'

Anatole looked mildly surprised. 'You were so devoted to her?'

Lyn swallowed. 'She needed someone to look after her. My mother—well, she wasn't very good at doing that. She'd ended up single, despite marrying twice, because both her husbands abandoned her. After that she spent most of her time in the pub, if I'm honest about it, and I didn't want Lindy to be a latchkey kid, so I stayed at home and did the housekeeping, cooking and so on. By the time Lindy left school Mum was ill. All the years of heavy smoking and drinking too much caught up with her finally, so I stayed to nurse her until the end. Lindy took a job in a wine bar and then, just after Mum died, took off with a girlfriend to London and lived in a flat share, worked in a flash West End wine bar. That's where she met your cousin.' She took a breath. 'When she realised she was pregnant she came back home, just as I was finally about to set off to university as a mature student. Of course I couldn't abandon her then...'

Anatole was silent a moment. A strange sense of recognition went through him. She had shouldered responsibilities not of her making—and he, too, was shouldering responsibilities he could have walked away from. Responsibilities that had brought him to this point: about to embark on a marriage to a woman he would never have known existed had it not been for the baby he'd set out to find...

But it was because of that baby—the baby who had stolen his heart already—that he was doing what he was doing now. The baby was all that was left of his young cousin, all the hope left to his ailing grandfather.

And I will see him right, whatever that takes!

His eyes went to the woman across the table from him. She'd opened up to him just now, more than she had yet done, so he knew he was making progress in gradually getting her to relax, getting her to feel less tense. Getting her to trust him.

He worked away at his goal assiduously, little by little making her feel more comfortable in his company.

Dinner on his second night back in London was a little easier than the preceding one. The main topic of conversation was Georgy, and Anatole could see that when Lyn talked about her nephew her eyes lit up, her face lost its pallor, and the animation in her expression made her seem noticeably more attractive. He found his curiosity as to what grooming and decent clothes might do for her intensifying. He found it curious that she seemed to be so reluctant to be made over. Most women, as he knew perfectly well, would have adored the prospect!

He'd backed off from pressing her the day before, when they'd been in the department store, but that evening he did no such thing.

'How did your swim go this afternoon?' he enquired at dinner, having spent the day working via his laptop. 'You said at breakfast you would take Georgy down to the pool. Did he enjoy the new pool toys we bought him?' he asked encouragingly.

Her reply confounded him.

'Um…the man at the desk said…' Lyn's voice tailed off. What the man at the desk had said still made her squirm.

Sorry, love. Pool's for residents only. Nannies don't count—even if they have their charges with them.

'Yes? The man at he desk said…?' Anatole prompted.

'Well, I think he thought I was Georgy's nanny,' she explained reluctantly.

An explosive noise came from Anatole and his expression darkened.

Immediately Lyn tried to mitigate the situation. 'It's very understandable,' she said. 'I know I don't look like I'm a resident here, so—'

'So *nothing*, Lyn!' Anatole's voice was firm. 'I trust you told the man who you were?'

She coloured. 'Um…no. It was a bit…a bit embarrassing. And I didn't want to make a fuss. He was only doing his job.'

He gave an exasperated sigh. 'Lyn, you must surely see that this cannot continue! Tomorrow I am taking you shopping for clothes and that is that!'

She nodded numbly. Clearly Anatole's patience was at an end. Well, she thought resolutely, not all rich women were beautiful, but they still wore expensive clothes. Now so would she.

'Good,' he said. He smiled at her encouragingly. 'Most women, Lyn, adore clothes-shopping!'

She gave a constrained smile in return, saying nothing. Thankfully, he let the topic go, and suggested they take their coffee into the lounge.

She set the coffee tray on a low table between the sofas and took a seat on the sofa opposite Anatole. He was wearing casual grey trousers and a beautiful soft cashmere jumper, the sleeves of which he now pushed back, revealing strong, tanned forearms. Immediately, Lyn made herself look away.

'Would you like any music?' she asked, for Anatole had not turned the TV on.

'Some Mozart, perhaps?' Anatole suggested, stretching out his arms along the back of the sofa and hooking one long leg casually over his thigh as he relaxed back.

The soft sweater stretched, moulding his torso. Punishingly conscious of his intense masculinity, she crossed to the music deck and made a suitable selection.

The scintillating tones of the *Linz Symphony* started to resonate through the room and she came back and resumed her place, curling her legs up under her and prudently removing several of Georgy's discarded toys from under various cushions, where he'd stuffed them earlier.

She leant forward to pour out the coffee. Black and unsweetened for Anatole. She knew that now. For herself, weak and milky. She proffered the cup to him and he reached a long arm forward to scoop it up.

As he did so his fingers touched hers. Jerking, she nearly dropped the saucer, but managed to avoid it, recoiling into her seat swiftly. She knew two spots of colour were in her cheeks. Covertly, she flicked her eyes across to the man opposite her. Large table lamps stood either side of the sofa, throwing a pool of soft light over him.

He is just so gorgeous-looking.

It dominated her consciousness, that constant awareness of his physical magnetism. A magnetism he seemed to be unconscious of himself. Or he just took it for granted, probably, she realised. If you grew up with looks like that you *did* take them for granted.

No wonder he wants me to look better than I do!

She bit her lip. Surely once she had got some smart clothes, done her hair, that sort of thing, she would look better than she did now? Not much, she knew dispiritedly, and certainly not enough to put her anywhere near Anatole's league, but surely better?

It was a hope that had to sustain her when, the next morning, back once again in the very swish department store in the West End they'd been to previously, Anatole went with her to the instore beauty salon.

'Hair and all the treatments first,' he told her decisively, 'then clothes and accessories. And while you're doing that…' he smiled reassuringly '…I'll take Georgy back to the Aladdin's Cave of the toy department.'

'He'll love that,' said Lyn, trying to hide her nervousness as the receptionist hovered, ready to usher her into the inner sanctum and the treatment rooms.

'When you're all done we'll go for lunch,' Anatole said, and then, with a final reassuring smile, he wheeled Georgy off.

'This way, madam,' said the receptionist, and Lyn was led away to her fate.

Anatole was enjoying himself. So was Georgy, nestled in the protective crook of Anatole's arm and gazing in open-mouthed delight at the miniature trains hurtling around the elaborate track layout of the vast display centrepiece of the store's toy department. Anatole was giving an explanation of the finer points of rail transport to him, which would probably have drawn indulgent amusement from the other shoppers present, being way too technical for a baby of Georgy's age, had it not been conducted in Greek.

Following Georgy's butterfly attention span, Anatole diverted towards the array of soft toys nearby, drawing the buggy along single-handed. A brief, if one-sided discussion with Georgy as to which soft toy he liked best of all resulted in Georgy becoming the highly satisfied owner of a floppy-limbed teddy bear almost as large as he was, and they set off for yet another circuit of the huge toy department. From time to time Anatole glanced at his watch, but he knew Lyn would not be ready yet.

What would she look like when she emerged? he wondered. He found it hard to envisage. He'd had little glimpses, sometimes, of what she *might* look like—when she wasn't looking tense and reserved and awkward.

But he wanted more than glimpses.

He glanced at his watch again impatiently.

'What about this one?' The stylist's voice was encouraging. 'It will turn heads,' she said enthusiastically, holding up a dress in fuchsia silk jersey.

Lyn stared uneasily.

Sensing it was too bright for her diffident client, the stylist immediately swapped the vivid dress for the same model in a soft coral instead.

'Or this one?' she asked.

'Um…OK,' said Lyn, nodding gratefully. Turning heads was not what she wanted to do—that was far too scary a thought.

But then this whole experience had been scary. For the last two hours she'd been subjected to one beauty treatment after another, and now—finally—with hair, nails and make-up all done, it was time to choose new clothes. The beautifully made dress slipped easily over her and the stylist got to work smoothing it and fastening it, then standing back to view her efforts. Lyn stood meekly, reluctant to look at herself in the mirror. A lot of effort had gone into improving her, and she was not at all sure about the results…

'Now—shoes,' said the stylist, and went to consult the trolley full of shoeboxes that had accompanied the dress rack. She pulled out a pair and held them momentarily against the fabric of the dress, then nodded. 'Yes, these are the ones.'

She helped Lyn into them, even though her client was looking at them, alarmed.

They had a high heel and a very narrow fitting. Yet they felt surprisingly comfortable on—presumably a sign of how scarily expensive they were. But it wasn't her place to object to any of this vast expenditure, so she said nothing. Nor did she say anything when she was presented with a matching clutch and, as a final touch, a piece of costume jewellery consisting of a couple of linked chunks of a copper-coloured stones was draped around her throat.

The stylist stepped back. 'There!' she exclaimed. 'Ready to roll.'

Even as she spoke another member of staff put her head around the door behind her. 'Mr Telonidis is at Reception,' she said.

'Just in time.' The stylist smiled at Lyn.

Stiltedly, Lyn smiled back. 'Um…thank you very much for everything,' she said.

'My pleasure,' said the woman.

Her voice was warm, and Lyn knew she was trying to be encouraging.

'I do hope you're pleased with the results.'

'The clothes and accessories are beautiful,' Lyn as-

sured her, feeling awkward. Then she turned away from
the window she'd been standing next to, doggedly staring out over the London skyline beyond, ready to go out
and face the man she was going to marry and hope—just
hope—that all the money he'd spent on her had not been
completely wasted!

As she turned a woman came into view and Lyn halted.
Where had *she* come from? She hadn't heard the door open
again. She must be the stylist's next client. Curiously, she
seemed to be wearing a very similar dress to the one the
woman had put on her. Maybe it was a favourite of the stylist's, she thought, confused. It certainly looked wonderful
on the other woman, with the soft neckline draping over
her bust and the dress lightly skimming her slim hips. The
total image was one of effortless chic, from her beautifully
cut hair to the elegant high heels and soft clutch handbag.

She gave herself a mental shake. She couldn't stand
here gawping. The other woman obviously wanted her
to vacate the room, as she was still standing there expectantly. Lyn took a step forward, wavering slightly on the
high heels she wasn't used to, and saw the woman step
towards her as well.

As if her brain cells were ungluing painfully, the truth
dawned on her.

Oh, my God, it's me!

She stopped dead, frozen and motionless. Just staring.
Her reflection—because of course, as her brain cells had
belatedly worked out, that was what it was—stared back.

The stylist was by the door, holding it open for her,
and numbly Lyn walked through and went out into the
reception area.

Anatole was there, leaning over Georgy in his buggy,
but he straightened as she emerged.

Then, in front of her eyes, he too froze. And stared.

'Lyn?' The disbelief in his voice was evident—he

couldn't hide it—but it was impossible to believe what his eyes were telling him. That the woman walking up to him had once been the drab, badly dressed female he'd handed over earlier. That woman was gone. Totally gone.

And she is never coming back!

The thought seared unbidden through his brain. Unbidden, but undeletable. That old version of Lyn was gone for ever! But this one—oh, *this* one could stay as long as she liked!

From deep inside him came an ancient, powerful emotion. Whatever it was that was calling it from him—the lissom lines of a figure he'd never had the faintest idea was underneath her old shapeless clothes, or the silky swing of freshly styled hair that had been released from its customary straggly knot and now skimmed her slender shoulders—his eyes narrowed infinitesimally as his masculine assessment moved to her face. Quite extraordinarily, the skilfully applied make-up now finally revealed her features—no longer muted but defined, enhanced…

Her eyes! Clear, wide-set, luminous. With delicately arched brows and their sockets softly deepened, the lashes richly lush. And her mouth—yet again Anatole felt all his male hormones kicking in powerfully—her mouth was as tender and inviting as a budding rose.

He murmured something in Greek. He didn't even know what it was, but it was repeating itself in his head as he finally gelled into movement. He stepped towards her and reached for her hand—the one that wasn't clutching a soft leather handbag as if it were a life-preserver—drew her towards him.

'You look fantastic!' he breathed.

His eyes worked over her. And over her again. Disbelief was still not quite dissipated. He took a step back again, and looked again still keeping her hand in his, try-

ing to take in what exactly had been done to her. It was…
everything! That was all he could think. Just…everything.

And yet it must have been there all along…

That was the most remarkable aspect of all. That underneath that wouldn't-look-once-let-alone-twice image
there had been *this* waiting to be revealed.

He went on staring—oblivious, for now, of the fact that
the expression on her face had reverted to the kind of stiff,
self-conscious, tense awkward one she had had right at the
beginning, when she hadn't been able to relax in his company even an iota.

Then, breaking into his studied scrutiny, he heard
Georgy demanding attention.

Dropping Anatole's hand, Lyn jerked forward. Thank
God for Georgy! Thank God for her being able to escape
that jet-powered, laser-intense gaze focused on her like
that…

She hunkered down beside Georgy and started to make
a fuss of him. Behind her Anatole finally surfaced and,
with a start, stepped towards the counter to settle up. As
he handed over his credit card it came to him that never
had his money been better spent. He turned back to Lyn
and another wash of disbelief hit him—followed by a very
strong male response.

'Time for lunch, I think,' he said as he took the buggy
handles and executed a neat turn of the wheels. His voice
was warm with satisfaction.

They lunched at the same swish restaurant they had before.
Anatole reckoned that Lyn would probably prefer a familiar place. Though this time she looked like a totally different woman! His feeling of satisfaction intensified. Yes,
he had done the right thing—absolutely the right thing—
in insisting on her having a makeover. To think that this
elegant, soigné woman he could not take his eyes off had

been there all along! He still found it hard to credit. What he did *not* find hard, however, was having her sitting opposite him like this. It meant he could study her in detail, take in every last dramatic improvement.

The only problem, to his mind, was that she seemed so ill at ease. He wondered why, and asked her right out.

She stared at him as if he had asked a really stupid question. Which, to her mind, he had. Of *course* she was feeling awkward and self-conscious! She'd felt that way when she'd looked awful—badly dressed and shabby—and now she felt that way when she looked the exact opposite! For exactly the same reason.

Because he makes me feel excruciatingly self-conscious all the time! Because I'm just so punishingly and constantly aware of how devastating he is! Because I just want to gaze and gaze at him, but I can't, because that would be the most embarrassing thing in all the world!

The stark truth blazed through her: Anatole Telonidis the man—not the millionaire, nor the man who was Georgy's father's cousin, nor the man she was marrying so she could keep the baby she adored—who sat there, effortlessly devastating from the top of his sable-haired head right down through the long, lean length of his body, was a man who could have an effect on her senses no other man had ever had.

That was why she could only sit there, quivering in every limb, unable to make eye contact, feeling so totally and utterly aware of him on every female frequency any woman could possess!

His sloe-dark expressive eyes were resting on her, expecting some kind of answer to his question. She had to say something. Anything.

'Um…' she managed, fiddling with her cutlery with fingers whose tips were now beautifully shaped with varnished nails. 'I guess I'm just getting used to being all dressed up like this.'

And to being stared at. Not just by you, but by everyone as I walked in here. And not just because we've got Georgy with us. This time they are staring at me, too, and I'm not used to it. It's never happened to me in my life before and I feel so, so conspicuous!

'You are not used to being beautiful,' Anatole answered, his expression softening. 'Don't poker up again. I said beautiful,' he told her, 'and I meant it.'

And he did, too. Her beauty, so newly revealed, was not flashy or flaunting. No, it was subtle and graceful. He wanted to gaze at it, study it.

Enjoy it.

But it was clear she was finding that difficult. Goodness knew why, but she was.

Ever mindful of her sensitivities, he made an effort to stop gazing at her, but it was almost impossible. Thoughts rippled through his head as he made that realisation, eddying and swirling out of the depths of his consciousness. Something was changing, something about the way he was thinking about her—but he couldn't give time to it. Not right now. He would think about it later. Right now he wanted her to feel comfortable. To enjoy lunch with him.

He gave her a smile. The kind he was used to giving her. Kindly and encouraging.

'What do you think you'd like to eat today?' he asked.

He started to go through the menu with her, and the exercise gave them both some time to regroup mentally. So did Georgy's requirements. He'd already had his lunch, in the children's café in the store's toy department. He'd relished it with enthusiasm—if rather more messily than Anatole had been prepared for. But he'd mopped up Georgy—and himself and the tabletop—manfully, and then purchased another top for him to wear, which he was now sporting colourfully. Spotting it, Lyn remarked upon it, and their conversation moved on to an account of Georgy's entertainment that morning.

'Sounds like you coped really well,' said Lyn. It was her turn to be encouraging. Having sole care of an infant could be quite a challenge, but Anatole was not shy of undertaking it.

'It's a delight to be with him,' Anatole said frankly.

He smiled, catching Lyn's eyes in mutual agreement, and a little rush went through her. Oh, Anatole might look like a Greek god, and be a high-powered millionaire business tycoon from a filthy-rich top-shelf Greek dynasty, but his loving fondness for his baby second cousin shone through! It was the one indisputable shared bond between them.

'A delight,' he repeated. 'But definitely full-on!'

'Oh, yes,' said Lyn meaningfully, glancing down at Georgy in his carrier, snoozing peacefully after all the excitement of the morning.

Anatole closed the leather-bound menu with a snap. 'After lunch,' he announced, 'we shall attend to the rest of your new wardrobe. There is a great deal to buy.'

She looked startled. Anatole reached across the table to take her hand. The delicately varnished nails glowed softly, and her skin was soft and warm. It felt good to hold her hand...

'Do not look so alarmed,' he said. 'It will be fine. I promise you. Trust me.'

She gazed at him. She was trusting him with so much already. Trusting him to ensure she could keep Georgy. Trusting him to sort out all the legalities. Trusting him to know the best way to ensure Georgy would never be wrenched from her.

With a little catch in her throat, she nodded. 'I will,' she said.

For a moment their eyes met, gazes held.

Then, with an answering nod, Anatole released her hand.

'Good,' he said. 'That's exactly what I want to hear.'

CHAPTER SEVEN

'IT'S A BEAUTIFUL day. Since we can't leave for Greece yet, let's go for a drive in the country,' Anatole announced.

His mood was good—very. It had been good ever since Lyn had walked out of the beauty salon looking so totally unlike the way she had looked before that he had scarcely been able to credit the transformation.

Now, as he smiled at her across the breakfast bar in the kitchen of the apartment, he still could hardly credit it. She was wearing one of the outfits they'd purchased the previous afternoon after their leisurely lunch, and it emphasised her amazing new look.

His eyes rested on her warmly. Georgy, securely fastened in his throne-like highchair, was waving a spoon around and blowing bubbles. But for once Anatole's primary concern was not Georgy. It was wondering just how Lyn had got away with looking so drab for so long when she could have looked the way she did this morning.

Her hair was clasped back into a loose ponytail, but the new style with its flattering colour tint made all the difference. So did the subtle, understated make-up she was wearing—little more than mascara and lipgloss, but all that was needed to turn her face from a collection of blank features into a face that had contours and depths. As for the sweater she was wearing—well, it was a million years away from the baggy items she'd used to hide herself in.

The soft lambswool jumper she had on, a light caramel, shaped her beautifully.

His eyes slid to her breasts. Before her makeover he'd never even noticed she had any.

But she does—she has beautiful rounded breasts. Slight, but well shaped...

Unbidden, the thought slid between his synapses.

What would she look like bare? Her slender body revealed to me? The sweet mounds of her breasts beneath my touch?

Joltingly he grabbed at his coffee. It was inappropriate to think in those terms.

Up till now he never had. But since her makeover those thoughts, questions, speculations had made themselves conscious in his head.

He pushed them aside.

'So, what do you think?' he said. 'Shall we get out of London today? Take Georgy out for the day?'

Lyn busied herself getting Georgy out of his highchair. The way Anatole was looking at her was making her colour.

I didn't know that was going to happen—I didn't think!

It was confusing—disturbing—to have his sloe-dark eyes resting on her like that. As if he was seeing her for the first time—for the first time as a woman...

Confusing—disturbing—making her blood pulse in her veins...

She forced her mind to focus on what he'd said—not on the effect his gaze was having on her, making her so self-conscious, making her body feel alive, somehow, in a way it never had been. Making her breasts feel fuller, rounder.

'That would be lovely!' she said brightly. 'Whereabouts do you want to go?'

'Heading south sounds good,' said Anatole.

And so it proved. Once across the girdle of the M25,

the North Downs behind them, the Weald stretched before
them. With Georgy safely secured in his car seat, Lyn was
seated in the passenger seat next to Anatole. She could feel
her eyes drawn to the way his strong hands were shaping
the wheel, his eyes focused on the road ahead. She wanted
to gaze at him, drink him in.

Instead, she made herself tell him what she knew about
this part of the country.

'It's called the Weald—from the Saxon word for forest—
like the German *Wald*,' she said. 'It's completely rural
now, but it was actually the industrial heartland of England for centuries.'

'How so?' Anatole asked, glancing at her. He wanted
to go on looking, because in profile she was well worth
looking at, but he had to keep his eyes on the road—which
he was finding a nuisance.

'The wood was used for charcoal, and that was used
for iron smelting,' she explained. 'And many of the trees
were cut down for shipbuilding as well.'

She went on to talk about some of the more notable
events in English history that had taken place in this part
of the country.

'Including the Battle of Hastings?' Anatole said knowl-
edgeably.

'Yes.' She sighed. 'The end of Anglo-Saxon England.
The Norman Yoke was harsh to begin with, imposed on
a conquered people.'

'Ah…' said Anatole, commiserating. 'Well, we Greeks
know about being conquered. We spent nearly four hundred years being ruled by the Ottoman Empire.'

The conversation moved to the subject of Greece's history as the powerful car ate up the miles. From the back
seat Georgy gazed contentedly out of the car window, but
when they pulled over at a pleasant-looking pub for lunch
he was ready to get out. The weather had warmed signif-

icantly, and they decided to risk eating in the garden—helped in their decision by the presence of a children's play area complete with sandpit.

'Don't let him eat the sand!' Lyn warned as Anatole lowered him onto its fine, dry golden surface.

'Georgy, a sensible boy never eats sand!' Anatole admonished him, as the baby rashly prepared to break this wise edict.

Memory stabbed at Lyn. In her head she heard Anatole similarly admonishing Georgy not to eat his watch, that first time he'd been with him.

How totally and irrevocably her life had changed since then!

I had no idea then that I would do what I have—that I would be here, now, like this, with him!

How far she had come since those first excruciatingly painful and awkward days as her life changed beyond recognition. Her eyes rested on Anatole now, hunkered down by the sandpit, engaging with his infant second cousin. Emotion went through her—and not just because of the sight of him and Georgy playing so happily, so naturally together. So much at ease.

She was at ease with him too now. Finding his company not fraught or awkward. Well, not in the same way, at any rate, she amended. Having her makeover had set off that intense awkwardness again, but she was getting used to her new look now. Finding it easier to cope with.

Enjoying it…

Because it was good to know she looked good! The novelty of it had lost its terror for her, leaving only pleasure. She'd caught sight of herself in the mirror in the ladies' here and a little ripple of pleasure had quivered through her. The designer jeans hugged her hips and thighs, the ankle boots, soft and comfortable, lengthened her legs, and the caramel lambswool jumper warmed and flattered her.

One of the young male servers came out and took their drinks order. His eyes, as he smiled down at Lyn, told her that she looked good to him too. That little ripple of pleasure came again.

From where he sat, Anatole watched Lyn interacting with the young man. It was good to see her being chilled about the effect she was having on the male population.

If she gets used to it from other men, she will get used to it from me too....

The words slid into his head and he busied himself with Georgy again, who was taking another lunge at the enticingly crunchy sand.

Lunch passed enjoyably, and afterwards they resumed their drive, finally reaching the South Downs. An airy walk on the high chalk expanse, with Georgy hoisted high on Anatole's shoulders, his little fists impaling his hair, laughing heartily, gave them some exercise. They paused at a viewpoint to look out and down over the blue glittering Channel beyond. Lyn tried to make out the coastal geography, hazarding some guesses as to what they were seeing.

'Do you know this part of England?' Anatole asked her.

'It has special memories for me,' she admitted.

Her gaze went out to the coast, and he saw a faraway look in her face—a look that was taking her back down the years.

'We came here on holiday once,' she told him. 'It was just about the only happy holiday I can remember. We stayed on a caravan park, right on the seashore, and Lindy and I were set loose to head down onto the beach every day. It was wonderful! We were so happy, I remember— so carefree! There were some beautiful houses at the far end of the bay, where the gardens opened right out onto the beach, and Lindy and I used to walk past them all and discuss which one we'd live in when we were grown up and had pots of money and no worries and cares.'

Anatole glanced at her. 'That sounds like you had a need for escapism,' he ventured, hoping she might say more.

It was good that she was starting to open up to him—to talk about her own life, herself, and Georgy's mother, too. He wanted to go on drawing her out. It was a sign that she was really starting to trust him, and he needed her to do that. The changes to her life he was imposing on her were so fundamental he did not want her shying away from them, panicking about what she was agreeing to do—bringing Georgy out to Greece and settling him there. So the more she confided in him, the more that trust would grow.

Lyn gave a little sigh. 'Yes, I suppose it *was* escapism, really. I remember that sometimes after that holiday, when things were particularly grim at home, I used to let myself fantasise that Lindy and I had run away to live in one of those lovely seaside houses on the beach—far away from the stress and strain of coping with Mum and all that went with her...'

'Was it *so* difficult when you were growing up?' he asked, his voice sympathetic.

She made a face. 'Well, I know many children have it loads, loads worse! But even so...for Lindy and me it was—well, difficult. That word you used fits the description.' She took a breath. 'Looking back, I can see that Mum probably suffered from depression. But whether it came from inside her, or whether it was because she couldn't really make a relationship last, I don't know. She'd have downers and take off for the pub, drown her sorrows. It's why I ended up more or less bringing up Lindy myself.' Her voice changed. Softened. 'Not that it wasn't a joy to do so. Lindy was always so sweet, so loving! And she had an infectious sense of humour—she could always set me laughing to cheer me up.'

Anatole saw a reminiscent smile cross her expression.

'What is it?' he probed. He let his gaze dwell on how, when she smiled, it lifted her features, lighting up her clear eyes and curving her tender mouth to show pearl-like teeth.

How could I ever have thought her unremarkable? If her sister had half her appeal Marcos must have been lost!

But, much as he might want to indulge himself in gazing at how her lovely smile enhanced the beauty that her makeover had revealed to him, he focused on her answer.

'The caravan park we stayed at was in a place called the Witterings,' Lyn explained. 'It's a pair of villages— East Wittering and West Wittering—and Lindy found the names hilarious! She only had to say them out loud and she fell into fits of giggles—and set me laughing too.'

There was fondness in her voice, and her expression had softened even more, but Anatole could see that faraway look in her eyes again—a shadow of the sadness that haunted her, at knowing her sister had barely made it into adulthood.

Let alone lived long enough to raise the child *they* were now caring for...

'We can go and visit there some time,' he said. 'If you would like?'

Lyn lifted her face to his. 'Can we? Oh, that would be lovely! I would love Georgy to know the place where his mother was happy as a child!'

He felt a spear of emotion go through him. As she gazed at him, her face alight, something moved inside him. He, too, longed for Georgy to know the beach by his grandfather's house, where he and Marcos had played as boys.

'We shall definitely do it,' he said decisively. 'Too far, alas, to include it in today's excursion, but we'll find an opportunity another day.'

He started walking again, and Lyn fell into stride beside him.

She must not let herself be endlessly sad for Lindy, she

knew that—knew that her beloved sister would not want it. Would want, instead, for Lyn to do everything within her power to ensure the son she hadn't been able to look after herself had the very best future possible!

Her eyes went to the man walking beside her. A stranger he might be, but with each day he was becoming less so—and, like her, he wanted only one thing: that Georgy should be kept safe, safe with them, not given to others to raise. And if that meant carrying out this extraordinary and unlikely plan of making a marriage between them, then she would see it through!

Marrying Anatole is the way I can keep Georgy safe with me—that's all I have to focus on!

Yet even as she repeated her mantra to herself she stole a glance sideways and felt her breath give a little catch that was nothing to do with the exertion of walking along these high, windswept downs and everything to do with the way she wanted to gaze and gaze at the compelling profile of the man beside her. At the way the wind was ruffling his sable hair, the way the sweep of his long lashes framed those sloe-dark eyes of his…and the way his long, strong legs strode effortlessly across the close-cropped turf, his hands curled around the chubby legs of Georgy, borne aloft on his wide shoulders.

He is just so incredible-looking!

The words burned in her consciousness and so too did the realisation that today—just as yesterday—she was finally looking like the kind of female a man like him would be seen with. Her style of looks might be quite different from Lindy's blonde prettiness, but she would have been lying if she had not accepted that with her new hairstyle, her new make-up and her beautiful new clothes she drew his approbation.

The transformation he had wrought in her appearance was just one more of the good things he was doing for her!

A sense of wellbeing infused in her and she heard scraps of poetry floating through her head as they walked the iconic landscape. The chalk Downs that ran along the southern coast of England plunged into the sea further east at Dover, and the peerless White Cliffs that defined the country. It was a landscape that had been celebrated a hundred years ago by one of England's most patriotic poets, Rudyard Kipling.

"'The Weald is good, the Downs are best—I'll give you the run of 'em, East to West,'" she exclaimed.

Anatole threw her an enquiring look and then his glance went down to her upturned face. Colour was flagged in her cheeks as the breeze crept up the steep scarp slope from the glittering Channel beyond. It lifted her hair from her face, and her eyes were shining as clear as the air they breathed. She seemed more alive than he had ever seen her. Vivid and vital.

And so very lovely.

A thought slid into his head. A thought that had been building for some time now. Ever since she'd walked out of the beauty salon and blown him away with the transformation in her looks. A thought that, once there, he could not banish. Found he did not want to banish. Wanted, instead, to savour…

Because why not? Why *not* do what he suddenly realised he very, very much wanted to do?

Why not, indeed?

He strode onward. Life seemed very good.

'What would you like to order for dinner?' Anatole enquired solicitously, strolling into the kitchen where Lyn was warming Georgy's bedtime milk.

'To be honest,' she said, 'I'd prefer something light. That cream tea we tucked into was very filling!'

They'd found an olde-worlde teashop in an olde-worlde

Sussex village to round off the day before setting off back to London, and Anatole found himself remembering the way she'd licked a tiny smear of cream from her lip with the tip of her tongue. He'd found it very engaging.

She was speaking again, and he made himself focus.

'If you want,' she ventured, her tone tentative, 'I could just knock up something simple for us both. Pasta or an omelette—something like that.'

His eyes smiled. 'Pasta sounds good. But I don't want to put you to any trouble.'

'No trouble,' she assured him.

'In exchange, I'll get Georgy off to sleep,' he volunteered.

'Thank you.' She smiled too.

He took the bottle from her and headed off.

She watched him go. It was so…contradictory. That was the only word she could find. On the one hand she felt so much easier now in his company. So much more relaxed. Yet on the other hand, since her makeover, 'relaxed' was the last thing she felt!

She felt as if a current of electricity were buzzing through her all the time—a current that soared whenever she saw him or he came near to her.

She took a breath. Well, hopefully, once they'd both got used to her new look it would dissipate—just as her initial stiltedness had.

It had better…

She gave her head a little shake and determinedly yanked open the door of the huge double fridge that occupied a sizeable space in the palatial kitchen. There were several bags of fresh pasta, as well as cream, eggs, butter and smoked salmon. A pot of fresh basil graced the windowsill by the sink, and she busied herself snipping at the fragrant leaves. By the time she had measured out the pasta, whisked some eggs, beaten cream in and chopped up the salmon, Anatole strolled back into the kitchen.

'Out like a light,' he said cheerfully. 'We clearly exhausted him today!' He crossed over to stand beside Lyn. 'Mmm…' he inspected her handiwork. 'Looking good.' He wandered across to the temperature controlled wine cabinet and extracted a bottle. 'I think this should wash it down nicely,' he said.

His mood was good. Very good. They'd had a good day out, Georgy had had fun, and he'd repaid their efforts by falling swiftly and soundly asleep. That left the evening to him and Lyn.

Yes, definitely a good day.

'You OK with eating in here?' he enquired.

'Yes, of course,' she assured him.

The breakfast bar was huge—plenty of room to dine at it. She heard him open the wine and got on with boiling a kettle of water to cook the pasta. Outside, the night sky was dark, but in the kitchen it felt cosy and companionable, warm and friendly.

Happiness filled her.

I didn't realise how lonely I've been since Lindy died…

But she was not lonely now. She had Anatole to be with.

Yet even as she thought that she felt a pang go through her. How long would they be together? This time next year it might very well all be over. His grandfather might have succumbed to his cancer, Georgy's adoption might be finally approved, and she and Anatole might have their mutually agreed divorce underway.

Somehow the thought chilled her.

'Why so sad?' Anatole's voice was kindly. 'Are you thinking of your sister?'

'Yes,' she lied. She poured boiling water into the pasta pan and fed in the spaghetti as it came back to the boil.

She did not want to look at Anatole. Did not want to let her eyes feast on him.

He isn't mine—he never will be. That's what I have to remember. The only thing I must remember.

Not the way her eyes followed him wherever he went. Not the way her breath caught when he smiled at her. Not the way she felt her pulse quicken when he came near her.

Not the way his face was imprinted on her mind, day and night...

'Then let us drink to her—and to my cousin, too.'

He slipped onto one of the high stools that flanked the kitchen bar. One of the ceiling spotlights caught the glint of pale gold in his glass as he lifted it, proffering the other one to Lyn as she took her place opposite him. They toasted their lost ones silently, each thinking their own thoughts about those they had loved who had died so tragically young.

'He wasn't all bad, you know—Marcos,' Anatole found himself saying. 'I know he treated your sister badly, but—well, I've come up with an explanation. It won't make you forgive him, but maybe you'll think of him a little less harshly.'

He looked across at Lyn.

'I think the reason he ignored your sister when she wrote to him is that he thought Timon would insist on him marrying her once he knew your sister was carrying his great-grandchild. Marcos was only twenty-five—and a young twenty-five at that. He wanted fun and no responsibilities. Timon encouraged him in that. He'd spent ten years trying to compensate Marcos for losing his parents at sixteen. A bad age to lose them. I think that learning that your sister was pregnant scared Marcos. Made him hide from it—hope it would all just go away.'

He looked at Lyn.

'I think that, had he not been killed, he would have

faced up to his responsibilities. He'd have come to me and told me first, I'm sure, and I would have helped him deal with it. Got him to make contact with Lindy. I believe,' he finished slowly, 'had your sister not died, he would have asked her to marry him. Made a family with her and Georgy just as she dreamed he would.' He paused again. 'He was a decent kid inside.'

Lyn heard him speak, felt her sympathy rising.

'It's all so sad,' she said. She was feeling choked. 'Just *so* sad.'

She felt her hand being taken, gently squeezed. 'Yes, it is. Sad and tragic and dreadful, and a hideous waste of young lives, their future stolen from them.'

She felt tears spring in her eyes. Felt Anatole's finger graze across her cheekbone, brushing them away. Felt his sympathy towards her.

'I hope they're happy together now, somehow. In that mysterious realm beyond mortal life. I hope,' he said, 'they're looking down at us and knowing their child is safe, his future assured.'

She nodded, blinking away her tears. He patted her hand and then, glancing at the stove, got up to drain the cooked pasta. She got to her feet as well, and busied herself stirring in the creamy concoction she'd prepared. She heaped it into wide pasta bowls and placed them on the bar. Her tears were gone now. Lindy was at peace and so, she hoped, was the man she'd fallen in love with. Who might one day, had they lived, have come to love her back.

Who knew? Who knew the mysteries of the heart? Who knew what life and fate and circumstance could do?

As she took her place opposite Anatole, letting her eyes savour him as they always did, she felt her heart swell.

Not with hope, for that would be impossible, but with a yearning that she could not still.

Anatole broke the moment and got to his feet. 'You

forgot the parmesan,' he said, and went to fetch it from the fridge.

It was such a simple meal, Lyn knew, but it was the most enjoyable she'd yet shared with Anatole. Despite her assurance that she was not very hungry she put away a good portion of pasta, and when Anatole extracted a tub of American ice cream from the freezer she did not disdain that either.

'Let's go next door,' he said, and led the way with the ice cream, leaving her to bring through the coffee tray.

She felt more relaxed than she had ever felt with him. The wine she'd drunk had helped, and it seemed to be giving her a very pleasant buzz in her veins. Carefully she set down the coffee tray and lowered herself onto the sofa beside Anatole as he indicated she should, taking one of the two long spoons he was holding out. He'd wrapped the ice cream carton in a teatowel, to make it easier to hold.

Sharing ice cream, Lyn swiftly discovered, meant getting a lot more up close and personal with Anatole than she'd initially realised. Digging into frozen ice cream was also, she discovered, enormously good fun when done in the right spirit.

'That lump of cookie dough is definitely mine!' Anatole informed her with mock severity. 'You had the last one!'

A giggle escaped her, and she made herself busy to focus on a hunk of chocolate in the icy mix.

'What would make this even more decadent,' Anatole observed, 'would be to pour a liqueur over it.'

'Or golden syrup,' contributed Lyn. 'Lindy and I used to do that as kids. The syrup goes really hard—it's great!' She stabbed at another bit of embedded cookie dough.

Finally, when they'd both OD'd on ice cream, they abandoned the carton and Lyn poured out the coffee. As she leant back, curling her legs underneath her into her usual posture, after handing Anatole's cup to him, she realised that his arm was stretched out along the back of the sofa. She could feel the warmth of his sleeve at the nape of her neck.

I ought to move further away from him, she thought. But she didn't. She just went on sitting there, feeling the heavy warmth of his arm behind her, sipping at her milky coffee.

'What's on TV?' Anatole asked.

Lyn clicked it on with the remote. The channel opened on one of her favourites—an old-fashioned, retro detective series, set back in the 1950s, just starting up.

She felt the arm behind her neck drape lower around her shoulders. He didn't seem to notice what he'd done, and for the life of her Lyn could not alter her position. She felt herself relax, so that her shoulder was almost nestled against him.

It felt good. It felt good to be almost snuggled up against him like this on the sofa, warm and well-fed, relaxed and rested.

Very good.

Another programme came on—this time a history show about the classical world. They watched with interest, Anatole contributing a little and Lyn listening avidly. He read out the Greek inscriptions on the monuments on show and translated them.

'Do you think you could face learning Greek?' he asked Lyn.

'I'll give it a go,' she said. 'The different alphabet will be a challenge, though.'

'It will come to you, I'm sure,' he said. 'I'll arrange lessons for you when we get there. Speaking of which,' he continued, 'it could be sooner than we think. The latest from the lawyers is that there's no objection to Georgy coming abroad with us, so his passport can be issued. We'll fly out as soon as we've got it.'

For a moment Lyn's eyes were veiled, her expression

troubled and unsure. The reality of taking Georgy to
Greece was hitting her. It would be soon now—very soon.

Anatole saw her doubts—saw the flicker of unease in
her expression. He knew she was remembering her old
fears about letting Georgy out of the UK to visit his father's family.

'It will be all right,' he said. 'I promise you. Trust me.'

She gazed into his dark eyes. He was right. She had to
trust him. He had done everything he had promised her he
would and she must do what she had undertaken. Go out to
Greece with Georgy, trusting the man who had taken the
responsibility of his care upon his own shoulders.

'I do trust you,' she whispered.

He smiled. 'Good,' he said.

Then, with a casual gesture, he moved her closer. She
nestled against him, his hand still cupping her shoulder,
as if it were the most natural thing in the world. She found
herself getting drowsy, the warmth of the room, the effect
of a couple of glasses of wine and the filling food all contributing. Her head sank back against his shoulder, her
eyes fluttering as she tried to keep them open.

'You're falling asleep,' Anatole murmured, glancing
sideways at her. He flicked off the TV programme.

She smiled drowsily. 'I'd better get Georgy's midnight
bottle going. He'll surface for it soon.'

'I'll get it,' said Anatole. 'You head for bed. I'll bring
the bottle in when it's warm.'

She uncurled herself and padded off. Five minutes later
she was propped up on the pillows, wearing her nightdress,
when Anatole entered with Georgy's milk.

'He's just waking up,' she said as he started to stir and
kick at his quilt. 'Up you come, then.' She lowered the side
of the cot and scooped him up.

'May I feed him?' Anatole requested, looking at Lyn.

'Yes, of course,' she said, slightly confused.

He moved to sit down beside her on the bed and she shuffled sideways against the edge of the cot, hastily putting a couple of pillows behind his back. He leant back, taking Georgy from her and settling him with the bottle. Lyn felt she should get up, but she was between Anatole and the cot. So she went on sitting there. Propped up. Shoulder to shoulder with Anatole. With only the low nightlight for illumination, the physical closeness between them felt very intimate.

Georgy sucked greedily and then, replete, let Lyn wind him gently before consenting to resume his slumbers in his cot. As she raised the side again, to lock it in place, she was burningly aware that Anatole was still beside her. She turned to make some kind of anodyne remark but the words died on her lips.

Anatole was looking at her with dark, deep, long-lashed eyes, his face half in shadow but the expression on it as clear as day. She felt her heart stop, her breathing stop. Everything stop.

Everything in the entire universe stopped except for one thing.

The slow dip of his head to hers. And then the slow, soft brush of his lips on hers. The slow rush of sensation it aroused.

'My lovely Lyn,' he murmured.

Then his kiss deepened.

His hand closed around her shoulder, covered only in the thin material of her nightdress. His hand felt warm and strong, kneading at her flesh as he turned her into his embrace. His mouth opened hers effortlessly, skilfully, and sensation exploded within her. Wonder and disbelief swept over her like a rushing wave.

Was this happening? Was this really, truly happening? Was Anatole kissing her? How could it be?

But it was—oh, it was. It *was*! His mouth was exploring

hers and his free hand was around the nape of her neck, moulding her to him. He was murmuring something in Greek that sounded honeyed and seductive. Warm fire lit within her, her senses flared…soared…and then suddenly he was sliding off the bed, taking her with him. Sweeping her up, striding out of the room with her in his arms, kissing her still.

She could say nothing, do nothing, only let him take her, carry her into his own bedroom, lower her down upon the bed's wide surface. She wanted to speak, to say something—anything—but it was beyond her. Totally beyond her.

He came down beside her, indenting the mattress with his long, lean length. His hands cupped her face as she gazed up at him.

'My lovely Lyn,' he said again. And his mouth came down on hers.

Helplessly, willingly, she gave herself to him, letting him ease her nightdress from her, letting his eyes, so deep and dark, feast on her form, letting his hands shape her breasts, glide along the lines of her flanks, slip under her back at her waist and half lift her to him with effortless strength. And all the while his lips worked their magic on hers, deepening the passion and the intensity.

She was in a state of bliss. Unable to think, to reason, to understand—able only to wonder, only to give herself to the sensations of her body, her yielding, arching body, which yearned and sought and found what she had never dreamed possible: the wonder of being embraced and caressed by this man.

Never had she thought it possible! Never had she dreamt of it in her wildest dreams! Yet now it was real—true. He was sweeping her to a place she had never imagined.

For how could imagination possibly have revealed to her what it would be like for Anatole to make love to her like this? Drawing from her, arousing in her, such incredible feelings that she could hardly keep her senses—so overwhelmed by his touch, his caresses, his sensuous, intimate kisses that sought and found her, every exquisitely sensitive place until her body was a living flame.

A flame that seared into the incandescence of quivering arousal as, stripping his clothes from his heated body, he came over her, his strongly muscled thighs pressing on her limbs, parting them. His hands closed around hers on either side of her head as his body—naked, glorious—arched over her, his questing mouth taking the honeyed sweetness of hers.

His eyes were hazed with desire, molten with urgency, as he lifted his head from her. She arched her hips towards his, yearning for the hot, crushing strength of his body. For one endless moment he held back, and then, with a triumphant surge, he filled her, fusing his body with hers, melding them,

She cried out—a high, unearthly sound—as sensation exploded through her. She heard his voice, hoarse and full-throated, felt the tips of her fingers indenting deeply, so deeply, into his sculpted back. Every muscle strained. Her hips arched against his.

It was like nothing she had ever experienced! It flooded through her, the whitest flame of ultimate consummation, further and further, reaching every cell in her body, flooding every synapse. She cried out again and the cry became a sob, emotion racking through her at the wonder of it, the beauty of it…

And then he was pulsing within her, and she was drawing him in, deeper and deeper, with more and more intensity of sensation, more wonderful yet, flowing and filling her like a molten tide. She clasped him to her, tightly and possessively, holding his body to her as, reaching its golden glowing limit, the tide began to ebb, drawing back through her body, releasing her from its wondrous thrall.

They lay together, their heated bodies limp now, sated, a tangle of limbs half wrapped around each other.

He cradled her to him, murmuring in his own language words she could not tell. But his hand was warm, splayed around the back of her head, holding her. Her breathing slowed and she felt an echoing slowing in him as well—a slackening of his embrace. Wonder washed like the sweetest wine through her fading consciousness as sleep finally overcame her, and she lay cradled and encircled within the embrace of his arms.

CHAPTER EIGHT

IT WAS THE distant, distressed crying of an infant that awoke her from heavy sleep. Fully waking, she heard Georgy's wailing. Instantly she was up, fumbling for her long-discarded nightdress and stumbling from the room towards her own. Stricken, she lifted his squalling body and clutched him tight. She never let him cry—*never*! Guilt smote her and she hugged him, swaying, soothing his little back until he eased, comforted and reassured finally that she was there and all was well. Slowly, very slowly, she eased him back into his cot, stroking his head.

A sound in the doorway made her turn. Anatole was there, naked but for a towel twisted around his hips, a questioning look on his face in the early light of the dawn.

'Is he all right?' he asked.

His voice was throaty, the timbre of it resonant.

She nodded dumbly as memory swept over her, hot and vivid. Dear God, had it really happened? Had she been swept off into Anatole's arms, his bed? Could it be real? True?

Then he was walking up to her, enfolding her in his arms.

'Come back to bed,' he said.

The voice was huskier than before. Its message clear.

Desire was in his eyes.

He kissed her. Soft, then not so soft. Slipped his hand into hers, leading her away…

Much, much later they surfaced.

This time they did not sleep. This time pale daylight edged past the folds of the curtains, proclaiming the day. She lay in the crook of Anatole's arm, half propped on soft pillows, drowsy. Fulfilled.

Hazed still with disbelief.

'Georgy will be waking,' she said. 'He'll be hungry.'

Anatole reached to the bedside table to glance at his watch. 'The day awaits,' he said. He turned back to kiss her softly. His eyes gazed down at her.

'My lovely Lyn,' he said. His eyes caressed her. 'So very lovely.'

Then, with a decisive movement, he threw back the coverings and got to his feet. His nudity was overwhelming, sending her senses into overdrive. Ruffling his hair, as if to wake himself further, he disappeared into the bathroom. Lyn hurried to her bedroom, swiftly showering before Georgy awoke.

In the shower, her body seemed fuller somehow—more rounded. She was still in a daze, yet it had happened. Her body felt it in every stretched and extended muscle, felt it in the warm, deep glow within her. Her breasts were crested, and she could see with amazed wonder the soft marks of his caressing.

As warm water sluiced over her, the shower gel gliding sensuously over her skin, she felt again the echo of the heat that had consumed her.

She dressed hurriedly, pulling on a pair of leggings and shouldering her way into a long, dark blue jersey wool top, loose and comfortable. She dried and brushed her hair out rapidly, not troubling to tie it back, and it tumbled around her shoulders—wavy, wanton. For a moment she caught sight of herself in one of the long wall mirrors in the room, and her reflection stayed her.

Her eyes glowed with sensual memory. Her breasts strained against the soft fabric of her top. She felt desire stir.

Then, with a rattle of cot bars, Georgy was pulling himself up to a sitting position and holding out his arms to her. With a smile, she scooped him up and out, and bore him off to the kitchen for his breakfast.

Anatole was there already, wearing a bathrobe, his hair still damp, fetching cereal and milk, and a baby yoghurt for Georgy. A sudden overpowering sense of shyness swept over Lyn. But he came towards her, bestowing a kiss on her cheek.

'Your tea is brewing,' he told her, smiling, and settled himself on a stool at the kitchen bar. He nodded at Georgy, still held in her arms. 'How is our infant prodigy today?' he enquired humorously.

Georgy responded to his attention by gurgling, and evincing a desire for his yoghurt, which he'd just spotted. Lyn took her seat, Georgy on her lap, and poured milk into her cup of tea, taking a first sip before reaching for the yoghurt. Somehow her shyness was gone.

'So,' said Anatole expansively, 'what shall we do today?'

He knew what he wanted to do. What he had wanted to do, he acknowledged, since the moment she'd walked out of the beauty salon, transformed and revealed. What had been building since then, hour by hour, until last night it had seemed the obvious, the only thing to do. Follow his awakened instincts to their natural fulfilling conclusion.

He was not about to question it, analyse it, challenge it. It was, after all, incredibly simple. Desire—simple and straightforward. And overwhelming.

Quite, quite overwhelming.

He had not expected it. He knew that. Had not thought that it would happen—*could* happen. But it had and he was glad of it! Totally, incredibly glad! It made sense on every level.

He let his gaze rest on her now. Georgy was snuggled on her lap as she spooned yoghurt into his gaping mouth, hungrily gulping it down, ready for more. Her features were soft, tender, as she smiled fondly at her charge.

Well-being filled him.

'How about,' he suggested, 'we take Georgy swimming this morning?'

It proved an excellent idea. Excellent not just because it was so enjoyable to see the fun that Georgy had—his little body safely held in the water with water wings, bobbing merrily as he chuckled gleefully at all the splashing, fully enthusiastic about the exciting inflatable pool toys acquired especially for him—but also because it afforded Anatole the considerable pleasure of seeing Lyn in one of the several new bathing costumes he'd insisted on her buying. True, it was a one-piece, but it was quite sufficiently revealing for him to feel desire stir all over again.

A desire that, when Georgy finally conceded defeat after lunch and succumbed to his nap, Anatole had no reason to defer any longer, and he swept Lyn off to bed.

'We have to take ruthless advantage of Georgy's sleep patterns,' he justified, overcoming Lyn's slight sense of shock at such diurnal amorousness.

But as she journeyed with him to that wondrous place of union she could only agree.

Anything that Anatole wanted was wonderful! Anything at all! She was ardent, adoring, her eyes lit with wonder and pleasure.

I can't think beyond this! It's impossible—impossible! All I can do is go with what is happening.

She was in a haze—a daze of happiness. And beyond each day, each night, she would not think.

Anatole walked out of his office to see Lyn sprawled on the floor with Georgy, who was on all fours, lurching forward in his newly developing crawl.

'The lawyers have just phoned me,' Anatole announced. He took a breath. 'Georgy's passport is being delivered by courier this morning. We fly to Athens tomorrow.'

He came to Lyn, whose eyes had flown up to his, and hunkered down beside her. Her expression was mixed.

'I know you are nervous,' he said, taking her hand and pressing it reassuringly, 'but once we are there you will find it less alarming, I promise you.'

His eyes met hers, but even as they did so they slid past, down to Georgy, intently progressing towards the teddy bear that Lyn had deliberately left out of his reach, to encourage him to try and crawl towards it. Thoughts swirled opaquely in his head. Thoughts he did not want to put into words. Thoughts he banished with the words he always used to reassure her.

'Trust me,' he said. He leant forward and brushed her mouth with his lightly. 'This is the right thing to do,' he said, his voice low, intense. 'It is the best way forward for Georgy—that is all you have to hold on to.'

Yet doubt, unease, still flickered in her face. He kissed her again, more deeply, and felt her shimmer with response. When he took his mouth away the doubt had gone from her eyes, replaced by the glow that was always in them when he kissed her, made love to her...

'That's better.' He smiled a warm, intimate smile and got to his feet. 'Now, do not worry about packing,' he instructed her. 'The maid service here will do that—both for you and for Georgy. We'll enjoy our last day here. Then, tomorrow, we'll be off!'

He headed from the room.

'I'm going to phone Timon—tell him we'll be there tomorrow and get an update from his doctors. They tell me the drugs are kicking in and starting to work, which is just the news I want.'

Lyn watched him go, and as he went from view she felt again that jittery feeling of unease return. It was such a big, frightening step—to leave the UK, to go to a foreign country and put herself entirely into the hands of a man who, such a short time ago, had been a stranger to her.

But Anatole was no longer a stranger! He was the man she had committed herself to with all her body, all her desire. He had swept her away on a wonderful, magical tide of passion and forged an intimacy between them that made a nonsense of her fears, her doubts.

Thanks to Anatole, everything would be for the best now.

Everything will be all right! I know it will! There is nothing to be afraid of—nothing! I must do what he keeps telling me to do—trust him!

And how could she fail to do so? How could she fail to trust him now that he had transformed her life? In his arms, his embrace, she had found a bliss that overwhelmed her with its wonder! There was no more awkwardness with him, no more shyness or diffidence.

Now everything between them was different! Magically, wonderfully different! Since Anatole had swept her into his arms, into his bed, her head had been in a constant daze. It was still so unbelievable, what had happened between them! So unbelievable that she could not make sense of it—could do nothing but simply go with it…with every wondrous, shining moment of it! She would allow herself no doubts, no questions.

The flight to Athens proved straightforward. Georgy took a keen interest in the proceedings, especially all the admiring fuss that was made of him by the cabin staff, and apart from being affected by the change in cabin pressure on take-off and landing had a smooth journey. At Athens airport they were whisked through deplaning and into the chauffeured car waiting for them. Lyn barely had time to take in her new surroundings before the car was leaving the airport, heading for the coast.

'It should take less than an hour, depending on traffic,' Anatole assured her. 'We'll have plenty of time to settle into the beach house this afternoon. As you know,' he went on, 'we have the whole place to ourselves—and I think that will be good. Give you a chance to get used to everything. With Timon still in hospital for the moment, under medical supervision, we can have more time together. That said—' he made a face '—I can't deny that I'm going to have to spend a great deal of time working. Both at my own affairs, which I've neglected, and even more importantly on Timon's business affairs.'

His expression tightened.

'My priority is persuading Timon to relinquish control of the Petranakos Corporation to me. I'm limited at the moment as to what I can and can't do, and I can see that a great deal needs to be done. A lot of the workforce at too many of the sites and premises are very jumpy—they know Timon is old and very ill, they know Marcos is dead, and they don't know what is going to happen. Bankers and investors are restless too, as well as suppliers and customers. None of that is good. I need to take charge—make it clear that I'm going to run the company on behalf of the new heir. And I most urgently want Timon to designate Georgy.' He took a breath. 'Whatever it takes, I *have* to get Timon to hand over the reins of power to me.'

Whatever it takes...

The words echoed in Anatole's head. He had used them so often in these past weeks since Marcos's fatal car crash.

His eyes went to the woman and child seated beside him and he felt them echo again.

Whatever it takes...

Emotion swirled within him. Whatever it took to safeguard Marcos's son and safeguard the jobs of the thousands of people employed by Timon. That was what he must cling to.

His mind refocusing, he started to point out to Lyn the various landmarks they were passing, giving her a sense of the geography of the region.

'We are heading for Glyfada,' he told her. 'It's on the shore of the Saronic Gulf—where, as I'm sure you already know, the famous battle of Salamis was fought in the fifth century BC to defeat the invading Persians. My grandfather's villa is beyond the resort, on a quiet peninsula, well away from all the glitz of Glyfada and its neighbours, like Voula.'

'I see the roadsigns are in the Latin alphabet, as well as Greek,' Lyn remarked.

'That's pretty common in Greece now,' Anatole reassured her.

She frowned. 'It's the hardest part of learning Greek, I think,' she said. 'Having to learn to read a different script.'

'It isn't so bad,' he said encouragingly. 'Lots of the symbols are the same. One or two can be confusing, though—like the Latin capital P, for example, which is our R: *rho*.' He smiled. 'But don't worry. You'll get the hang of it. I'll get a teacher organised, and you can start lessons as soon as you like.'

'Thank you,' she said gratefully. Her heart warmed. He was taking so much trouble to make her feel easier, more comfortable about moving here to Greece.

Yet even so, as the car turned off the main highway, and started to head down smaller roads, threading between what were clearly private and expensive residences

all around them then pausing to go through electronically
controlled gates to curl around a driveway that led to the
huge white villa at the far end, Lyn felt her heart quail
again.

But yet again Anatole sought to assuage her fears as she
stared, daunted, at the massive ornate mansion.

'Timon likes to live in style,' Anatole commented dryly.
'But the beach house is a lot less grandiose.'

The car took a fork off to the right that went around
the main house and down through extensive manicured
grounds that led towards the sea, and drew up outside a
much more modest-looking building.

'This will be far more suitable for us,' said Anatole.

Lyn could not help but agree.

It was a single-storey, low-level building, with shutters
and a terrace to the front, which overlooked the far end
of a private beach that fronted the shoreline of the main
villa, from which it was separated by formal gardens set
with tall cypress trees and a lot of cultivated greenery.

'I've had the beach house opened up, but no one's been
here for a while, so it might be a bit musty,' Anatole apol-
ogized.

Lyn only smiled. 'It looks lovely,' she said. She definitely felt relieved that she wouldn't have to cope with the
huge imposing-looking villa that was Timon Petranokos's
residence.

They made their way indoors, leaving the driver to
bring in their luggage. Indoors, Lyn immediately felt even
more reassured. Although it was clearly a luxury residence
the house was small-scale, and simply furnished, but she
liked it that way.

'The staff from the main house will do the housekeeping here,' Anatole explained, 'and the kitchen there will
always be on call. Tonight,' he went on, 'we'll definitely
make use of my grandfather's chef!'

Lyn was grateful, and by the time she had sorted out her unpacking and got Georgy settled in his new nursery in the bedroom next to hers, she was glad to sit down to a dinner that someone else had prepared.

She still felt strange, but knew she must simply get on with settling in. This was to be her life now.

But for how long?

The thought arrowed through her head and she wished it had not. She didn't want to think about the future right now.

All she wanted to do was be with Georgy—and Anatole…

With Anatole's arms around her, his lips kissing her, his hands caressing her, his words murmuring in her ear as he took her to a place that made everything else in the universe disappear…

She wouldn't think about anything else. Just what she had now.

Take each day…each night…and do what he asks you to do. Trust him.

It was all she needed to do.

The following morning they drove to the specialist cancer hospital outside Athens where Timon Petranakos was being treated.

'I hope you do not mind, Lyn,' Anatole said, 'but for this first meeting I want to take Georgy to see Timon on his own.'

Lyn was understanding. 'Of course,' she agreed readily.

It was understandable that he should want that. This would be a very emotional encounter for a man, old and dying, who, still raw with terrible grief, had lost his beloved grandson but who now was to receive a blessing he had never hoped for: his grandson's baby son. She did not wish to intrude on such a special moment.

Anatole was tense, she could see. So much was rest-ing on this encounter, and she did not want to add to that tension. She leant across to give Georgy, already hoisted up in Anatole's arms, a quick final mop of the face, ready to be presented to his great-grandfather, then she stood back, watching Anatole walk out of the visitors' lounge at the swish private clinic. As the door closed behind them, taking Georgy from her sight, a little bubble of anxiety formed inside her. She deflated it swiftly.

What did she imagine was going to happen? That a frail, sick man like Timon was somehow going to whisk Georgy away, never to be seen by her again? Of course he wasn't! She must stop fretting like this. Just as Anatole kept reit-erating, everything would be all right...

She sat back on the chair and reached for a magazine to while away the time until Anatole emerged again. She could do little but glance at the pictures, and it strength-ened her determination to get to grips with the Greek lan-guage without delay. This might only be the first day after their arrival, but the sooner she could cope with the lan-guage the better.

It was a determination she found she had ample time to put into practice in the days that followed. Anatole had warned her that once in Greece he would have to focus primarily on work so, like it or not, she had to wave good-bye to him in the mornings as he headed into Athens, leav-ing her to her own devices during the day. Not that she had any housework to do—maids from the main house appeared and duly disappeared after taking care of all the chores, and food shopping was also taken care of by Timon Petranakos's staff. They all made a huge fuss over Georgy, who clearly revelled in the admiration, and those who spoke English told her, with visible emotion, how like his poor tragic father he was. She herself was treated with great deference as well, as the fiancée of Timon's other grandson, which she found a little awkward. It brought home to her the very different worlds she and Anatole came from.

But it doesn't matter—we are united in Georgy. He bridges any gap between us.

Not that there *was* any gap. She might not see anything of Anatole during the day, but when he came home in the evening he was everything she could desire.

She'd made a point of cooking dinner herself some evenings, for she was reluctant to rely totally on Timon's house staff to do so for her, but she knew her meagre repertoire would soon pall for someone like Anatole, used to gourmet cuisine all his life, so she restricted herself to easy dishes like pasta, leaving anything more complex to the chef from the main house. Baby food, though, she attended to herself, and soon discovered that shopping for fresh fruit and vegetables with Georgy in the nearby little coastal town—to which she was delivered and collected by Timon's chauffeur—made for a pleasurable excursion every day or two. The Greeks, she swiftly realised, were a lot more volubly enthusiastic about infants than the reserved British, and everyone from passing old ladies to shopkeepers made a huge fuss of him whenever she wheeled him along in his buggy, much to his evident enjoyment.

Having bought herself some teach-yourself and tourist phrasebooks for Greek, Lyn steadily tried to put her first stumbling efforts with the language into use as she shopped. They were aided when the teacher Anatole had promised he would organise arrived at the beach house. He was an earnest young man—the graduate son of the brother of Anatole's PA—and with his assiduous help Lyn started to feel less intimated by the Greek script, started to make definite progress with grammar and vocabulary.

While she had her daily lesson one of the housemaids

would look after Georgy. She spoke to him in Greek, as did Anatole quite a lot, and Lyn knew that it was essential that he grow up to be bilingual from the start—a tangible sign of his dual heritage.

But she also knew she didn't want him growing up unaware or under-exposed to his mother's heritage too. It was something that caused her some anxiety now that she was actually here in Greece. It might not matter while Georgy was little, but as he grew to boyhood Lyn knew she would want him to be as much English as Greek. She owed it to Lindy…

She said as much one evening to Anatole over dinner. She felt a little awkward raising the subject, but steeled herself to slip it into the conversation at an opportune moment. He had made some remark about their day out to the South Downs while they'd been in England, and Lyn seized her chance.

'We *will* be able to go back to England some time?' she asked. 'I know we'll have to go back after the wedding at some point, to be present at the adoption hearing, but once that is done do we come back here for good?'

For a moment he stilled completely, and she realised he might have misunderstood her question.

His eyes rested on her. 'Are you not happy here?' he asked.

There was a concerned note in his voice and immediately Lyn replied. 'No, it's not because of that at all—I promise you! I'm settling in, just as you promised me I would! Please, *please* don't worry about that! You've got enough to deal with as it is—with Timon's state of health and all the work you've got to do! I suppose it's simply dawning on me that once Georgy starts talking he's going to have Greek as his predominant language and culture—and I don't want him to lose touch with his English side completely. It would be reassuring to know that he can spend time in England, still—for holidays…that sort of thing! Touch base with that side of his cultural heritage.' She finished hastily. 'But that's all for the future, I know.'

'Yes, it is,' said Anatole. 'But of course I can see why you think about it.' He took a breath. 'We can work something out, I am sure,' he said.

There was reassurance in his voice, but suddenly Lyn saw a veil come down over his expression, as if he were thinking of something he was not telling her about.

She frowned inwardly, and a thread of anxiety plucked at her. It dissipated almost immediately, however, as Anatole's expression cleared.

'I'm going to try and take the day off tomorrow,' he said. 'What's that expression in English? Playing hockey?'

Lyn laughed. 'It's playing *hookey*—but I have no idea what hookey is, or why you play it when you skive off work!'

Anatole gave a quirking smile. *'Skive?'* he queried.

'It's slang for bunking off—which is also slang for going AWOL, I guess…taking a day off work when really you're not supposed to.'

'Well, I think I deserve it,' Anatole said firmly. 'I've been flat out since we got here, and the pressure is only going to get worse when I'm running Petranakos fully. For the moment I'm going to take a long weekend for once.' He looked at Lyn. 'How about if I take you into Athens and show you the sights? I feel bad that you've been stuck away here and haven't seen anything yet.'

Lyn's face lit. 'Oh, that would be wonderful! Thank you! But please, *please* don't feel I've been "stuck" here—this is such a lovely house, with the beach right in front, and the weather is so lovely and warm.'

Anatole looked at her. 'Are you sure you're happy here, Lyn?' he asked.

She could hear the concern in his voice again, and immediately wanted to reassure him. 'Yes, truly I am! It's getting less strange every day. And so is the language.'

'Good,' said Anatole, and relief was clear in his eyes. 'The other good news is that Timon's oncologist tells me he's continuing to do well. The cancer is responding to the drugs and he is coping better with the side effects. He's talking about letting him come home next week, maybe.' His eyes warmed. 'And then, Lyn, we can really get going on our wedding.'

His gaze caressed her, and she felt herself melt as she always did.

'Not that we need to wait for the wedding...' he murmured, and his message was clear—and potent.

Lyn felt a little shimmer as her blood warmed. No, they did not need the formality of a wedding to unite them. It might be needed to expedite the adoption process, which was still progressing back in the UK, but she and Anatole needed no marriage lines to release the passion between them!

Happiness welled through her.

She had everything she could ever dream of here with Anatole, in his arms, in the life he had made for her here with her beloved Georgy!

And if there was a shadow over her happiness, over the future that was yet to come—well, she would not think about that now. Would not let herself be haunted by it.

She would give herself only to the present—this wonderful, magical present that Anatole had created for her!

'There's something else the oncologist was saying, Lyn.'

Anatole's voice penetrated her haze of happiness. She brought her mind back smartly.

'He thinks that Timon is now sufficiently strong to receive visitors—I mean beyond just me and Georgy. I know you've been very understanding that Timon has really not felt up to coping with meeting you yet, and you know how brief I've had to keep my own visits to him, but of course he is keen to meet you. So…' He took a breath. 'How about if on our way into Athens tomorrow we go via the clinic? How would that be?'

His expression was encouraging, and Lyn knew she must acquiesce. She might have her own apprehension about finally meeting Georgy's formidable great-grandfather, the patriarch of the family, but it was something that had to be faced some time. And tomorrow, after all, was as good a day as any.

She dressed the next morning with particular care, and was conscious of a feeling of tension as they arrived at the clinic—conscious, too, of Anatole's warm, strong hand holding hers as they went indoors, dissipating her tension. Georgy was in her arms, and was already a clear favourite with the reception staff, and with the nurse who escorted them to Timon's room.

Anatole went in first, just to check his grandfather was ready for the encounter, and a moment later emerged to escort Lyn inside. He took Georgy from her, hefting him easily into his strong arms, and guided Lyn forward.

'Lyn—come and meet my grandfather,' he said.

She stepped towards the bed, her eyes going to the occupant. So this, she thought, was Timon Petranakos.

A lion of a man, she realised, but one on whom old age, grief and extreme illness had taken a heavy toll. Yet his eyes, as dark as Anatole's, held her with a penetrating regard. For a moment he said nothing, simply looked at her as if taking her measure. Then he nodded.

'It is good to meet you,' he said. His voice was somewhat rasping, and his accent in English strong.

'How do you do?' she said politely.

He gave a short, rasping laugh. 'Not well, but better than I might.' His dark eyes turned to Georgy, who was blowing bubbles at him from Anatole's arms. 'And all the better for seeing *you*!'

He switched to Greek, bestowing what Lyn took to be words of warm affection for Georgy and holding out his gnarled hands for Anatole to place him on his lap. She watched them interact—the old, sick man who had lost both son and grandson before their time and the infant who represented to him all the hope he had for the future. Anatole joined in, speaking Greek as well, and making a fuss of Georgy, who clearly loved being the centre of attention.

Lyn stood at the foot of the bed, feeling suddenly awkward.

Excluded.

Then, abruptly, Timon's head lifted. 'Tell me about his mother,' he commanded.

And it definitely *was* a command, she realised. But she made allowances. A man of his generation, his wealth, the head of a powerful Greek family, would be used to giving commands to all around him.

She swallowed, wondering what to say, where to begin. 'Lindy was…the sweetest person you could know,' she said. 'Loving and gentle.'

It hurt to talk about her, and yet she was glad that Timon Petranakos was asking.

'Beautiful?' he probed.

She nodded. 'Blonde and blue eyed,' she answered.

The short, rasping laugh came again. 'No wonder my Marcos wanted her! He had good taste, that grandson of mine!' There was an obvious note of indulgence in his voice as he talked about Georgy's father. Then the dark eyes went to his other grandson, seated beside him. 'As does this grandson too,' he added.

His gaze slid back to Lyn, and she felt herself flushing slightly. She dropped her eyes, feeling awkward.

'So,' Timon went on, 'you have the wedding all prepared, the two of you?'

Was there something different about his voice as he threw that at them? Lyn wondered uneasily. But perhaps it was just the thickness of his accent.

Anatole was answering him. 'We want you to be out of here first. Back at home.'

Timon nodded. 'Well, the wretches who are my doctors tell me that another week should make that possible.' His eyes went back to Lyn. For a moment there was that measuring expression in them again, and then his face creased into a smile.

'We are going into the city after we have left you,' said Anatole. 'Lyn wants to see the sights.'

Timon's eyes lit. 'Athens is the cradle of civilisation,' he told Lyn. 'No city in the world can compare to it!' His eyes went to his great-grandson. 'It would be unthinkable for Marcos's son to grow up anywhere else. *Unthinkable!*'

'Well,' said Anatole, 'that is what we are making possible.'

He nodded at his grandfather and said something to him in Greek that she did not understand. It was probably, she thought, something to do with the legal issues surrounding Georgy's adoption, because Timon answered in an impatient tone, to which Anatole gave a reply that seemed to have a warning note to it. Lyn could understand how Antole's grandfather might feel irked by the ponderous and exhaustive bureaucracy of the adoption process.

Then Timon's dark, sunken eyes were turned on her again, and once more Lyn felt herself being measured—assessed. She made herself hold the penetrating gaze, though, returning it with a clear, transparent expression. Abruptly Timon's lined face broke into a smile and he nodded.

'Good, good,' he said, in his strong accent. Then he

lifted a hand. 'Go—go, the pair of you.' He turned towards Anatole. 'Take her into the city. Buy her things she likes,' he instructed.

A nurse came bustling in, telling them that Kyrios Petranakos needed to rest now and take his medication. Anatole got to his feet, scooping up Georgy with him. He spoke affectionately to his grandfather in Greek, then came to Lyn as they made their farewells. Lyn was conscious of a feeling of slight relief as they left. Timon Petranakos might be old and ill, but there was an aura of power about him that meant it was more comfortable being out of his presence, however kindly he had been towards her.

As they settled back into the car and set off for the city centre Anatole looked across at Lyn.

'Not too bad, was it?' he asked, cocking an eyebrow at her. But his eyes had a sympathetic glint in them.

'He is quite formidable,' she allowed.

Anatole nodded in agreement. 'He is of his generation,' he said. 'As he demonstrates,' he added dryly, 'by his belief that the way to win a woman over is to "buy her things she likes…"'

Lyn couldn't help but smile. 'You don't have to buy me anything!' she said. Her expression changed as she gazed at him. 'And you've won me over anyway, already—totally and completely!'

His eyes caught hers. 'Have I?' he said softly

'You know you have…' she breathed, her eyes and face alight with everything she felt for him.

He reached across Georgy's infant seat and lightly, so lightly, brushed Lyn's mouth.

'Good,' he said. Then he sat back.

Just for a moment Lyn thought she could see in his air and attitude the same aura of satisfaction she'd seen in Timon's smile.

Well, why not? Anatole is his grandson—of course there will be physical similarities!

Then Georgy was patting at her arm, wanting her attention. She gave it instantly and fully, as she always did, for never, *ever* would she dream of neglecting him—not even for Anatole.

The day they spent in Athens was magical for Lyn. Timon Petranakos had spoken the truth—the city *was*, indeed, the cradle of civilisation, the birthplace of democracy. As they made their way up to the Parthenon Anatole regaled her with millennia of history.

'How extraordinary,' Lyn said as they stood and gazed at the peerless ancient monument that had withstood all the centuries had thrown at it, 'to think that in this very place your ancestors came to worship! Two and half *thousand* years ago!'

Anatole gave his wry smile. 'We take it for granted sometimes and forget how much history we have compared with many other nations.'

She hooked her hand into his arm. 'You'd never run out of history here if you were a student,' she said.

He glanced across at her. 'Tell me,' he asked, 'if I could track down a suitable course of historical study would you be interested in taking it?'

She looked at him doubtfully. 'In Greek?' she asked. 'I don't think I'm anywhere near being able to cope with that.'

Anatole shook his head. 'I'm sure there must be courses in English. The British School at Athens, for example, runs English language summer courses in archaeology, I seem to remember. There are probably other opportunities as well—I'm sure we could find something that would suit you. After all, history was what you originally wanted to study before you had to divert to accountancy.'

'It would be wonderful if I could have a go at history

again!' she enthused. Then she frowned slightly. 'But I don't think it's practical now I'm looking after Georgy.'

Anatole looked at her with his familiar amused expression. 'Lyn—it's one of the many perks of wealth that childcare can easily be sorted! Speaking of which…' His tone of voice changed again, and Lyn looked at him. 'Timon was telling me that he wants to provide us with a nanny for Georgy.'

She looked startled. 'What for?' she said blankly.

He made a slight face. 'Like I said, he is of his generation. To him it is natural for children to be looked after by nursemaids and nannies.'

'I don't *want* to hand Georgy over to nursemaids and nannies!' Lyn exclaimed.

Anatole kissed her forehead. 'Don't worry about it, Lyn.' His tone of voice changed again. 'Now, do you feel up to visiting the temple of Nike as well? Or shall we take a coffee break first?'

They continued with their excursion, and Anatole regaled Lyn with everything he knew about all the monuments they were seeing. By the time they were finished Lyn was glad to set off back home again.

She looked at Anatole as they settled back into the car. 'It will most definitely take more than one visit to see everything in Athens!' she said with a smile.

'In the summer it will get too hot for sightseeing,' he replied, 'so it's best to see as much as possible now, while it's still relatively cool.' He smiled. 'We can drive in again tomorrow, if you like, or if you prefer we could drive out and see more of Attica itself—the whole region that Athens is set in.'

'Oh, that would be lovely!' enthused Lyn.

So they took off the next morning, with Anatole driving this time, touring through the Greek landscape, eating lunch at a little vine-shaded *taverna*, then heading for the majestic temple of Poseidon at Sounion, which stood in breathtaking splendour on the edge of the sea.

The following day they took a launch across the Saronic Gulf to the holiday island of Aegina, and spent a relaxed day there.

It was bliss, Lyn thought happily, to have Anatole all to herself—to spend the day with him, enjoying Georgy between them. Happiness ran like a warm current through her—a contentment such as she had never known. Walking, chatting comfortably, eating ice cream, Georgy aloft on Anatole's shoulders as they strolled along the seafront— it seemed to her so natural, so right.

We're like a real family...

That was what it felt like. She knew it did! And if there were to come a time when they would no longer be united like this for Georgy's sake then it was something she did not want to think about. Not now—not yet.

For now all she wanted to do was give herself to what she had, what there was between them—which was so, *so* much! For now this was enough. This happiness that bathed her in a glow as warm as the sunshine...

CHAPTER NINE

TIMON ARRIVED HOME from hospital at the end of the following week in a private ambulance and with his own large personal nursing team. Anatole had escorted him from the clinic, and when he was safely installed in his master bedroom, with all the medical equipment around him, Lyn brought Georgy in to visit him.

This second visit was less intimidating, and although Timon was polite and courteous to her most of his attention was, understandably, focused on his great-grandson. Now that he was back in his palatial mansion she would wheel Georgy up through the gardens to visit him every day, Lyn resolved.

The following day Anatole arrived back from Athens earlier in the evening than usual.

'We've been summoned,' he told Lyn wryly, kissing her in greeting. 'Timon wants us to dine with him.'

Lyn frowned slightly. 'What about Georgy? He'll be in bed by then.'

'One of the maids can babysit,' answered Anatole, heading for the shower room. 'Oh, and Lyn…' His voice had changed. 'I'm afraid Timon has gone ahead with hiring a nanny for us.'

She stared after him in some consternation.

Immediately he continued, 'Please don't be anxious— she will be based up at the villa, not here, and she will only be for our convenience. Nothing else. Such as for evenings like this.'

Lyn bit her tongue. It wasn't an outrageous thing for Timon to have done, but it was unsettling all the same. And she would have preferred to have had some say in just who the nanny would be. Timon's ideas were likely to run to the kind of old-fashioned, starchy, uniformed nanny who liked to have sole charge of her infant and keep parents— adoptive or otherwise—well at bay.

But she put her disquiet aside. She would deal with it after their wedding—which was approaching fast now that Timon was out of hospital. This time next week she and Anatole would be husband and wife. A little thrill went through her—a bubble of emotion that warmed her veins. But with it came, yet again, that sense of plucking at her heartstrings that always came when she let herself think beyond the present.

This time next week we'll be married—and this time next year we might be already divorced...

She felt her heart squeeze, her throat constrict.

Don't think about this time next year—don't think about anything but what you have now! Which is so much more than you ever dreamed possible!

With a little shake she went to get ready herself for going up to the big house and dining in what she was pretty sure would be a much more formal style than she and Anatole adopted here in the little beach villa.

And so it proved.

Timon might still be an invalid, and in a wheelchair, but he commanded the head of the table in the huge, opulently appointed dining room as he must surely have done all his life. The meal was as opulent as the decor, with multiple courses and an array of staff hovering to place plates and refill glasses. Though she did her best, Lyn could not but help feeling if not intimidated, then definitely ill-at-ease.

It didn't help matters that Timon focused most of his conversational energies on Anatole, and that the main subject under discussion appeared to be a situation that was developing at one of the Petranakos factories in Thessaloniki, in the north of Greece.

Anatole elaborated a little to her, in English, as the meal progressed. 'The workers there are on short time already,' he said to her, 'and now the manager is issuing redundancies. It's not proving popular, as you can imagine.'

'Redundancies are unavoidable!' snapped Timon, interjecting brusquely.

Anatole turned back to him. 'It's been badly handled,' he said bluntly. 'Without any consultation, discussion or explanation. The manager there should be replaced.'

'He's *my* appointment,' growled Timon.

Anatole's mouth set, but he said nothing.

Timon's dark eyes flashed as they rested on his grandson. 'You're not in charge of Petranakos yet!' he exclaimed. 'And I don't *have* to put you in charge, I'll have you remember—'

He changed to Greek, speaking rapidly, with little emotion, and then broke off as a coughing fit overcame him. Lyn sat awkwardly, aware of the strong currents flowing between grandfather and grandson. Anatole looked tense, and she longed to smooth away his worries.

She got her chance when they got back to the beach house finally. After checking on Georgy, thanking the maid who'd babysat and sending her off back to the big house, she went into the kitchen to make Anatole his customary late-night coffee. When she took it into the bedroom he was already in bed, sitting back against the pillows, his laptop open on his knees. He glanced at Lyn, gratefully taking the coffee.

'I ought to be glad that Timon is—very clearly!—feeling better, but I have to say,' he went on darkly, 'it's making him reluctant to relinquish his chairman's role to me.' He made a wry face. 'The trouble is his management style is not suited to the current dire economic conditions. It's out of touch, too authoritarian, and that's far too inflammatory right now!' He took a mouthful of coffee. 'I need to get him to resign from chairing the executive board and put me in his place, so I can sort things out properly, in a more conciliatory fashion, without having all the employees up in arms! But Timon's proving stubborn about it!'

Lyn knelt beside him and started working at the knots in his shoulders.

Anatole rolled his head appreciatively. He caught her hand. 'I'm sorry this is erupting now,' he told her, 'so close to the wedding. But if things don't calm down in Thessaloniki soon I may have to go there. And,' he finished, his mouth tightening, 'I am going to have to do whatever it takes to persuade Timon to hand over the reins of power to me irrevocably! Too much is at stake! He says he wants to wait until Georgy's adoption is confirmed—but I can't wait till then now that all this has flared up. If the workers in Thessaloniki come out on strike it will cost the company millions in the end! I have to stop it getting that far, and to do that I need to have free rein to take what action is necessary!' He took a breath. 'I'm going to tackle Timon tomorrow. Get him to agree to the handover finally!'

He set down his coffee cup, turned off his laptop, and wrapped an arm around Lyn.

'The next few days are going to be tough,' he warned her apologetically. 'It's going to be a race against time to get everything sorted out before the wedding.' He gave a heavy sigh. 'I'll have to be up early tomorrow, just to tell you in advance, and you won't see much of me for the rest of the week, I'm afraid. It makes sense for me to stay in my apartment in Athens until the weekend. There's even a chance that the situation in Thessaloniki will require me to fly up there myself now. I hope not, but I'd better warn you about the possibility all the same.'

Lyn felt a little stab of dismay at the thought of being without Anatole, but knew she must not add to the heavy pressure on him already by showing it. Instead she put on a sympathetic smile and kissed his cheek.

'Poor you,' she said. 'I hope it turns out all right.'

'Me too,' he agreed.

His eyes started to close, and Lyn reached to put out the light. Tonight, sleep was clearly on the agenda.

But in just over a week we'll be on our honeymoon! she reminded herself.

That little thrill of emotion came again as she settled herself down, nestling against the already sleeping Anatole. She wrapped an arm around him, holding him close.

Very close…

'Right, then, Georgy my lad—no use us sitting here moping!' Lyn instructed her nephew and herself roundly as she carried him through into the bathroom to get dressed and ready for the day.

She'd woken to discover that Anatole had, as he had warned her, taken himself off at the crack of dawn to get to his desk, and she had immediately felt her spirits flatten at the dispiriting prospect of his absence for several days to come. Sternly, she'd admonished herself for her craven wish that Anatole were not so diligent in the execution of his responsibilities towards Timon's affairs. She had dramatic testimony that it was those very qualities that she had so much reason to be grateful for. It was, she knew, totally *because* Anatole had such a strong sense of responsibility that he had undertaken so drastic a course of action in safeguarding Georgy's future.

Marrying me! Bringing me here to live with him, with Georgy! Making a home for us here!

Automatically she felt her cheeks glow. He'd done so much more than that!

He's transformed me—transformed my life! Given me a wondrous happiness that I never knew existed! In his arms I have found a bliss that takes my breath away!

Her eyes lit with the light that was always in them when she thought of Anatole and how wonderful he was—how wonderful it was to be here with him.

To think I once feared that he would take Georgy from me! To think that I wished he had never discovered his existence—never come into my life!

Because it was impossible to think that now! Utterly impossible! With every passing day, every hour spent with him, her gratitude and her happiness increased beyond measure! He was doing everything to make her feel comfortable here in Greece, to make her feel at home…valued and cherished.

His concern for her, his solicitude, his thoughtfulness, were all so precious to her!

With deft swiftness she got Georgy ready, then followed suit for herself. It was another warm sunny day, and even if she wished that she could look forward to Anatole coming home, however late he might be, she would not let her spirits sink. She had another Greek lesson in the afternoon, and she was making steady progress in the language—both speaking and reading it. She thought ahead. In the evening she would busy herself reading some of the hefty history books about Greece that Anatole had provided her with in English. She was determined to be as informed as possible when she applied to the history studies course Anatole had suggested she take after the summer.

A little glow filled her again. He was so thoughtful! Despite being rushed off his feet at work he had still found time to think about what she might like to do after they were married, getting her brain engaged again and not neglecting her love of history.

To think that, were it not for him, I'd be stuck studying accountancy and facing making a living endlessly totting up rows and rows of dull figures! I can study at my leisure, study the subject I love most, and it's all thanks to Anatole!

She headed downstairs with Georgy, telling him just how wonderful his big second cousin was—information that her nephew received with equanimity and a familiar chortle. When they reached the kitchen he wriggled in her arms to be set down, but then, as she was about to settle him into his highchair, ready for breakfast, something caught his eye.

It caught Lyn's too.

It was a package on the kitchen table, set in the place she usually sat. It was wrapped in gold coloured wrapping paper and bound up with a huge silver bow. Puzzled, she went round the table to look at it. Georgy immediately lunged for the enticing bow, and she had to busy herself getting him secure in his chair and then hastily unfastening the bow and presenting it to him. He did what he always liked doing best, which was to cram it straight in his mouth to sample. She let him do so absent-mindedly as she undid the rest of the wrapping.

Inside the gold paper was a document case—a tooled leather one—and on the top of it was a card. She lifted it and turned it over. Anatole's familiar handwriting leapt at her.

Timon instructed me to buy you things you like—I hope this fits the bill.

Curious, emotions running, she opened the document case and withdrew its contents.

She gasped.

Attached to some thick, headed paper was a photograph of a house.

An obviously English house in mellow brick, with roses round the door, set in a lovely English garden. In the foreground was a white picket fence, into which a little wicket gate had been set. The photo, she suddenly realised, had been taken from the wide strip of sand onto which the wicket gate opened.

Memory shot through her.

And a spear of emotion with it!

She knew exactly where this house was—exactly where the photo must have been taken! In her head she heard herself telling Anatole about when she had first seen houses like this one.

'Lindy and I used to walk past them all and discuss which one we'd live in...'

She picked up the photo and stared at it. This was certainly one of the prettiest she and Lindy must have seen!

Her eyes dropped to the rest of the contents of the document case and then widened in disbelief. With a catch in her throat she lifted them up.

It was a set of title deeds—deeds to the house whose photo she was gazing at.

Deeds made out to *her*...

Incredulously she let go of the papers, her hands flying to her face, not believing what she was seeing. Yet it was there—all there in black and white. The formal headings and the language was telling her that *she* was the owner of the house in the photo...

She gave a little cry and her eyes lit upon a note clipped to the corner of the deeds. It was in Anatole's handwriting. She picked it up and stared at it, emotion lighting within her.

'So you can always have a place you love in England for yourself.'

'Oh—*Anatole*!' she exclaimed. Incredulity went through her and through her—along with wonder and a wash of gratitude. She could not believe it—for him to have done such a thing for *her*!

She rushed to find her mobile and with fumbling fingers texted him straight away.

It's the most wonderful surprise—and you are the most wonderful man in the world! Thank you, thank you, thank you!

Moments later a reply arrived.

Glad you like it—in haste, A

For the rest of the day she was in a daze of wonder and happiness. If she had thought it a sign of his solicitude and care for her that he wanted her not to neglect her studies, *this* incredible act of generosity and concern overwhelmed her!

That Anatole had taken to heart her concerns that Georgy should not lose all his English heritage—and even more, that he had remembered her telling him about her seaside holiday with Lindy, a precious little island of carefree happiness in a difficult childhood—was a shining testimony to just how wonderful he was!

How am I going to bear divorcing him?

The thought sprang into her head unbidden—unwelcome and unwanted—and she felt it stab at her. She had got used to trying to keep it at bay, for with every passing day spent in her new and wonderful life she knew she was finding the prospect of just how temporary their forthcoming marriage was supposed to be increasingly unwelcome. How simple it had sounded when she had first let herself be drawn into this drastic solution to safeguard Georgy!

But things are now completely and totally different from then! Never in a million years did I imagine just how my relationship with Anatole would be transformed by him! Now the last thing I want to do is for us to part...

The cold wash of knowing that at some point in the future Anatole would extract himself from their marriage, conclude what had never been intended to be anything more than a temporary arrangement solely to enable them to adopt Georgy and settle him out here in Greece, chilled her to the bone.

Words, thoughts, sprang hectically in her brain.

I don't want us to part! I don't want us to go our separate ways, make separate lives for ourselves! I don't. I don't!

She gazed at Georgy, anguish in her eyes.

I want to go on as we are, being together, bringing up Georgy together, making our lives together...

Her face worked.

Maybe Anatole does too! That's what I have to hope— that he is finding the life we are making here as good as I do! That he is happy, and does not want us to change anything, for us to divorce and go our separate ways...

She could feel hope squeezing at her heart—hope and longing.

Let it be so—oh, please, please let it be so!

Didn't that incredible gift of his—the fantastic gift to her of a house of her own, where she could take Georgy sometimes to walk in the footsteps of his mother—show all his generosity, all his thoughtfulness? Wasn't that tangible proof of how much he felt for her?

And how easy it was to spend time with him—how comfortably they chatted and talked! That was good, wasn't it? It must be, surely? And the way they could laugh together, too, and smile at Georgy's antics...

And Georgy—oh, Georgy was beloved by them both. How doting they were to him, how dedicated!

A quiver of fire ran down her veins as she thought of the passion they exchanged night after night, the incredible desire she had for him, that he too must feel for her. Surely that most of all must tell her that what they had between them was not something unreal, temporary, that could be turned off like a tap?

Oh, please, let me mean as much to Anatole as he does to me... Please let it be so!

Anatole rubbed at his eyes as he sat at Timon's huge desk at Petranakos headquarters. God, he could do with some sleep! He was used to working hard, but this was punishing. Non-stop, just about, for the last four days on end. And nights. Nights spent here in Athens, at his apartment. He didn't like to leave Lyn and Georgy at the beach house, but there had been no option. Now that he'd finally got the chairmanship of the whole Petranakos Corporation, with full executive powers, there was a huge amount to do, on far too many fronts, at the huge, complex organisation that would one day be Georgy's.

The deteriorating situation in Thessaloniki was the most pressing, but by no means the only one. For with Timon having been hospitalised until so recently, daily management had become lax in many quarters. Even so, the threatened strike was requiring the bulk of his attention. So much so that he knew he was going to be hard-pressed to find the time to do something even more vital.

Get out of Athens tonight and back to Lyn—to talk to her.

Talk to her as quickly and as urgently as possible. The day of their wedding was approaching fast, and he could hear the clock ticking. He was running out of time.

Tonight—tonight I'll sit her down and tell her.

Tell her what he *must* tell her without any further delay

He glanced at the document lying in its folder at the side of his desk. It had been delivered to him by courier only an hour before. It seemed to lie there like a heavy weight on the mahogany surface of Timon Petranakos's desk.

For a moment Anatole's face blanked. Had he done the right thing?

Yes! I didn't have a choice. I had to do it! It's the reason I undertook this whole business—right from the very moment of reading those sad, pleading letters to Marcos...

The phone rang on his desk, cutting dead his thoughts, and he snatched it up. Now what?

A moment later he knew—and his expression said it all. Face black, he pushed back Timon's huge leather chair, packed away his laptop in his briefcase and strode out of the office. Timon's PA looked up expectantly.

'Put the jet on standby. I'm flying up to Thessaloniki,' he barked.

Then he was gone.

Lyn was both pleased and surprised to receive a call from Anatole in the middle of the day. But she quickly realised that the call was serious rather than tender. He told her that he was calling from his car on the way to the airport, just to let her know what was happening.

'I'll keep this brief,' he went on crisply. 'I'm going to have to fly up to Thessaloniki right away. A strike has just been declared, there's a mass walk-out, and protests are building outside the factory gates. The riot police have been marshalled by the manager—just what I don't need!' He took a heavy breath. 'But at least—finally!—I've got the power to sort it out myself.' He paused. 'I don't know when I'm going to be able to get back, Lyn.' His voice changed suddenly. 'And I have to talk to you urgently the moment I do.'

'What is it?' Alarm filled her throat.

She heard him give a rasp of frustration at the other end of their connection. 'I need to explain to you face-to-face. But, listen, please—I hope you'll understand—'

He broke off. Lyn heard a staccato burst of conversation in Greek, then Anatole was audible again.

'I'm sorry! I have to go. I'm flying up with the chief finance director and he's just heard on his own phone that there's been a clash with police outside the factory—and that TV crews are arriving to film it! I've got to speak to the officer in charge and get the police to back off for the moment. This can't escalate any further!'

The connection went dead.

Dismay filled Lyn. Not just at the fracas that Anatole was going to have to deal with, but because of what he'd just said to her—that he needed to talk to her urgently.

He had sounded so sombre…

What's wrong?

The question burned in her head but she could find no answer. It went on burning even as she crossed to the TV and turned to the Greek news channel. Even without understanding much Greek she could see that the angry dispute at the Petranakos facility in Thessaloniki was making the headlines.

If you want to help Anatole let him get on with sorting it out without making any demands on him yourself! she told herself sternly.

She'd done her best to do that for the past few days. Yet the beach house felt lonely without him. Their bed empty…

Worse, when she set off for the main house later, with Georgy in his buggy, for his daily visit to his great-grandfather, she was intercepted by a uniformed woman who informed her that she was Georgy's new nanny.

'I will take Baby to Kyrios Petranakos,' she announced in accented English.

Lyn hesitated. She didn't want this to happen, but this was not the moment to make a fuss, she knew. Reluctantly, she let the nanny take Georgy from her.

'I will bring him home later,' the nanny said punctiliously, with a smile that Lyn made herself *not* think of as condescending.

She shook her head. 'No, that's all right. I'll wait.'

She went out into the gardens and settled herself on a little bench in the sunshine. Despite the warmth, she felt chilled. Clearly Timon, now that he was back home again, wanted to make his presence felt—and to arrange things the way he liked them.

Well, she would wait until after the wedding—when Anatole was not having to deal with a strike on his hands—to take issue over the nanny and agree just what her role and function would be, if any. For now she would be accommodating. Bothering Anatole with something so trivial when he was up to his eyes in trying to sort out a costly and disruptive strike was the last thing she wanted to do!

She clung to that resolve now, knowing that he had flown up to Thessaloniki to deal with the problem there first-hand. But another concern was plucking at her. Would Anatole even be back in time for the wedding? And, even if he were, would they be able to get away on honeymoon at all?

Well, like the nanny situation, there was nothing she could do about it right now. Their wedding was going to be small and private anyway, and only a civil one since both parties knew it was going to end in divorce at some point, so there would be no guests to unarrange. On top of that, because Timon and Anatole were still in mourning for Marcos, it would have been inappropriate to have a large wedding anyway. So, Lyn made herself reason, if the wedding had to be postponed for the time being, and the honeymoon too—well, that was that. Anatole would sort out the strike, find a resolution that kept everyone happy, then come back home again. Then they would marry, and everything would be all right.

While their marriage lasted...

That chill formed again around her heart. She didn't want to think about the terms of their marriage—didn't want to think how it was supposed to end once Timon was no more. Didn't want to think about how, at some point, Anatole would divorce her and they would make suitable, civilised arrangements to share custody of Georgy...

Suitable. Civilised.

Such cold-blooded words—nothing like the passion that flared between her and Anatole! Nothing like the emotion that swept through her as he swept her into his arms...

She closed her eyes a moment, swaying slightly.

If only...

Words formed in her head—tantalising, yearning.

If only this marriage were not just for Georgy's sake...

She made herself breathe out sharply. She must not think such thoughts! This marriage *was* for Georgy's sake— that was the truth of it. And anything else—anything that had happened between her and Anatole—could not last any longer than their marriage...

It could not.

However much she yearned for it to do so...

CHAPTER TEN

She woke the next day in low spirits to the sound of Georgy grizzling in his cot. His grumpy mood seemed to echo her own lowness, and nothing could divert him. She got through most of the morning somehow, restricting her urge to phone Anatole and merely sending him an upbeat e-mail, assuring him that everything was fine on her end and refraining from expressing her own down mood or mentioning Georgy's tetchiness. By early afternoon she was glad to be able to set off with Georgy to the big house, for at least it gave him something to think about other than his grouchiness. Maybe he was starting to teethe, she thought. Whatever it was, he was not a happy bunny—and nor was she.

She eked out their expedition to the big house, first wheeling Georgy along the shoreline and pointing out things that might cheer him up, and then, giving up on that, heading into the gardens towards the house. She took a meandering route, not caring if she were running late.

When she duly presented herself the new nanny did not come forward to remove Georgy from his buggy. Instead she gave Lyn a tight smile and informed her that she would take Baby for a stroll in the gardens.

'Kyrios Petranakos wishes to see you without Baby,' she announced loftily, and took the buggy handles from Lyn.

'Oh,' said Lyn, feeling mildly surprised and mildly apprehensive.

What could Timon Petranakos want? she thought. She reasoned it must be something to do with the forthcoming wedding.

Oh, please don't say it's going to have to be postponed because of all that's going on in Thessaloniki!

She took a breath. Well, if it had to be postponed, so be it. Anatole was under quite enough pressure as it was.

She let the nanny wheel Georgy away, warning her that he was a bit grouchy today and getting a condescending smile in return, and then set off after the manservant who was conducting her to Timon's quarters. When she was shown in he was in his day room, next door to his bedchamber—a huge room with the same ornate, opulent decor as the dining room that Lyn found a tad oppressive and overdone, but she appreciated it was a bygone style suitable for a man of his age and position in society.

When she was shown in his wheelchair was in front of his desk and he was clearly studying the documents laid out on it. He wheeled the motorised chair around to face her as the manservant backed out of the room, leaving Lyn facing Georgy's great-grandfather.

There was something different about him. At first she thought it was something to do with his state of health, but then she realised it was his expression.

Especially his eyes.

They were resting on her, but the brief, penetrating glance she'd got used to was now a more focused stare. She stood still, letting him look her over. Somewhere deep inside her, unease was forming.

What was going on?

With a hideous plunging of her heart, she heard her voice blurting out, 'Has something happened to Anatole?'

Dear God, was *that* what this was about? Had something happened to him? Something to do with the protest, violent clashes?

Please don't let him be injured! Or worse...

Fear pooled like acid in her stomach.

'Yes—something has happened to Anatole.'

She heard Timon's words and faintness drummed through her. Then, at his next words, her head cleared.

Brutally.

As brutally as the harsh words came from Timon Petranakos in his hoarse voice.

'Anatole is free—finally free. Of *you!*'

She stared. 'What do you mean?' she said, a confused expression filling her face.

A rasp came from him, and she could see his clawed hand clench the arm of his wheelchair.

'I mean what I say!' he ground out. 'My grandson is free of *you!*' His expression changed, his eyes hardening like flint. '*Hah!* You stare at me as if you cannot believe me! Well, believe me!' The dark eyes pinioned her. 'Did you really think,' he ground out, his accent becoming stronger with the emotion that was so clearly visible in his lined face, 'that I would permit him to be trapped by *you*?'

Lyn's face worked, her senses reeling.

'I...I...don't understand,' she said again. It sounded limp, but it was all she could think right now. What was happening? Dear God, what was *happening*? It was like being hit by a tsunami—a wall of denunciation that she had never expected! Never thought to receive! Her mind recoiled and she clutched at flying words and thoughts to try desperately, urgently, to make some kind of sense of them! Find some kind of reason for what was going on here.

Timon's jaw set. The flint in his eyes, sunken as they were with age and illness, hardened.

'Then understand *this*, if you please! Your dreams of being Kyria Telonidis are over! *Over!*'

A little cry came from her throat, tearing it like a raw wound. She wanted to speak, shout, yell, but she couldn't—not a single word. She was silenced. Helpless to make sense of any of this—anything at all!

Timon was speaking again, his voice harsh and accusing. His words cut at her, slashing into her.

'You thought to trap him. You took one look at him and thought you had it made. Thought you could use *my* grandson's boy to trap my other grandson! To land yourself a life of ease and luxury that you have *no* right to! None! You saw your opportunity to make a wealthy marriage and a lucrative divorce and you took it!'

The bitter eyes flashed like knives, stabbing into her.

Shock spiked her riposte. 'Anatole *offered* to marry me—it was *his* idea, not mine! He said it would make it easier to adopt Georgy—I agreed for Georgy's sake!' Lyn tried to fight back, tried to stand her ground in the face of this onslaught.

Timon's face twisted in anger. 'For your *own* sake!'

'No!' she cried out desperately. 'It isn't like that! It's for Georgy! It's all for Georgy!'

The lined face hardened. 'Then you will be overjoyed to realise that you have achieved that! Marcos's boy is here now—in the country where he belongs—and whatever those infernal, interfering, officious bureaucrats in England say, no court in Greece will hand him back. No court in Greece will take *my great-grandson* from me! And as for you—know that for all your scheming you have been well served in turn!' His expression twisted. 'Did you truly think that because Anatole took you to his bed he would actually go through with *marrying* you? He did it to keep you sweet—and it achieved his purpose—to get Marcos's boy here the quickest way!'

'No! I don't believe it! *No!*' She covered her ears with

her hands, as if she could blot out the hateful, hideous words.

'Well, believe it!' Timon snarled at her. 'Believe it to be justice served upon you—justice for your scheming, for your lies!'

She froze, her hands falling inert to her sides. Her face paled. 'What do you mean—lies?'

His dark eyes glittered with venom. 'Ah—*now* she is caught! Yes—*lies*! The lies you've told Anatole...'

Her face paled. 'I...I don't understand...' Her voice faltered.

A claw-like hand lifted a piece of paper from his desk and held it up. Gimlet eyes bored into her. 'Did you think I would not have you investigated? The woman who stood between me and my great-grandson? Of course I did!' His voice changed, became chilled. 'And how very right I was to do so.'

As if weights were pulling at them her eyes dropped to the paper in his hand. She could read the letterhead, read the name of an investigative firm, read the brief opening paragraph with her name in it...

She felt sick, her stomach clenching.

'You don't understand...' she said. But her voice was like a thread.

'I understand *completely*!' Timon Petranakos threw back at her, dropping the paper to the desk.

Lyn's hands were clenching and unclenching. She forced herself to shift her gaze to the dark, unforgiving eyes upon her. The claws in her stomach worked.

'Have...have you told Anatole?'

It was the one question burning in her veins.

A rasp came from Timon. 'What do *you* think?' he exclaimed, and she could hear the bitterness in his voice, the anger.

'I can explain—' she started, but he cut her off with another harsh rasp of his voice.

'To what purpose? You lied to Anatole and now you are caught out! It is justice upon your head—nothing more than justice that all your schemes were always going to be in vain! That you were never going to achieve your ambition to marry my grandson, enrich yourself for life! And use *my* great-grandson to do it! Well...' He threw his head back, eyes raking her like talons. 'Your schemes are over now!' The claw-like hand reached for another paper on his desk, and thrust it at her. 'Look—*look!* And see how all your schemes have come to nothing!'

She felt her arm reach out, her fingers close nervelessly on the thick document that Timon was thrusting at her. It was typed in Greek, with a printed heading, and the unfamiliar characters blurred and resolved. It looked formal—legal—and she could not read a word of it. But at the base was a date—two days ago—and, above it a signature.

Anatole Telonidis.

Timon was speaking again. 'Here is a translation,' he said. 'I had it drawn up for you. For just this moment.' He lifted another piece of paper. The layout was exactly the same as the Greek document, but this was in English. Only the signature at its base was absent. With trembling hands she took the paper, held it up. Again the words blurred, would not resolve themselves.

'Keep it,' said Timon Petranokos. 'Keep them both. This document gives Anatole everything he wants—everything he's been asking for! He has taken over as chairman. Total control. Full executive power. I've given it to him. And all he had to do to get what he wanted,' he went on, the dark, sunken eyes glittering with animosity, 'was undertake not to marry you.' He paused. 'He signed it without hesitation,' he finished harshly, his mouth twisting.

He took another rasping, difficult breath, as if so much speaking had drained him of his scarce reserves of energy.

She should pity him, Lyn thought, but she could not.

She could only fear him.

But fear was no use to her now. It hadn't been when Lindy had died. It hadn't been when the social workers had sought to take Georgy for adoption. It hadn't been when Anatole Telonidis had turned up, dropping his bomb-shell into her life about Georgy's dead father and the vast fortune he would inherit one day from his dying great-grandfather—the fortune Anatole was now safeguarding for Georgy by agreeing to what his grandfather demanded: shedding the bride-to-be he did not want...

Had never wanted.

It was like a spear in her side, hearing those words in her head—a spear that pierced her to her very core! Her vision flickered and she felt her heart slamming in her chest, her lungs bereft of oxygen. She gasped to breathe.

Timon was speaking again, vituperation in his voice. 'So you see there is nothing here for you now. *Nothing!* All there is for you to do is pack your bags and go! Take your-self off!' His dark eyes were filled with loathing. 'Your lies have come to nothing! And nothing is all that you de-serve! To get rid of you as fast as I can do so I will hand you this, to speed you on your way!'

He thrust yet one more piece of paper at her—a small one this time—the size of a cheque.

'Take it!' he rasped.

Lyn stared at it blindly, frozen. She couldn't think, couldn't function—could only feel. Feel blow after blow landing upon her. Hammering her with pain. But she must not feel pain. Must not allow herself to do so. Later she would feel it, but not now. Now, at this moment, pain was unimportant. Only her next words were important.

To buy time.

Time to *think*, to work out what she must do—whatever it took—to keep Georgy safe with her.

She took a breath, tortured and ragged, forced her features to become uncontorted. Forced herself to think, to do something—anything other than just stand there while she reeled with what was happening.

She lifted her head. Stared straight at Timon. She should pity him—old and dying as he was, with his beloved grandson Marcos dead and buried so short a time ago. But she could not—not now. All she could do was what she was forcing herself to do now. To reach her hand out jerkily, as if it were being forced by an alien power, and take the cheque he offered.

She was at the beach house, staring at her mobile on which sat an unread text from Anatole, which had arrived while she was out having her life smashed to pieces. Beside the laptop on the dining room table were the documents Timon had thrust upon her and her Greek dictionary open beside them. Her frail and desperate hope that the translation he had given her was a lie had died. As she had slowly, painfully forced herself to read the original version, with Anatole's signature on it, word by damning word her last hope had withered to nothing

Anatole had done exactly what Timon had told her he had done. He had taken control of the Petranakos Corporation with full powers, just as he had always aimed to do.

Lyn's insides hollowed with pain. And he had done what he had always intended to do with her too. *Always*—right from the start! It was obvious now—hideously, crucifyingly obvious!

Not marry me—

A choking breathlessness filled her. The air was sucked from her lungs, suffocating her with horror.

*He was never going to marry me! Never! It was a lie—
all along!*

And now he did not need to lie any more. There was no
need for it. No need for any more pretence, any more charade.

As she sat there staring at the damning evidence the
phone rang. For a moment, with a jolt, she thought it was
her mobile, then she realised it was the landline. Almost
she ignored it, but it went on and on, so with nerveless fingers she picked it up.

It was not Anatole. It was a voice speaking to her in
Greek and immediately changing to English when the
speaker heard her halting reply. It was an official from
the town hall, confirming that the wedding due to take
place in four days' time was indeed, as requested by Kyrios
Telonidis via e-mail the previous day, cancelled.

She set down the phone. There was no emotion left
within her. None at all. She could not allow any—must
not—dared not. She stared back at her mobile, at the unread text from Anatole. She pressed her finger down to
open it. To read her fate. She stared as the words entered
her brain.

Lyn, I'm cancelling the wedding. I need to talk to you. Urgently. Be there when I phone tonight. A

She went on staring. Numbness filled her the way it
had filled her when she'd sat beside Lindy's dead body, all
the life gone out of it. All hope gone. Then slowly she got
to her feet, picking up the damning documents, looking
around her at the place she had thought so *stupidly* was
going to be her home…

The home she'd share with Anatole.

The man who had just cancelled their wedding.

Not just postponed—but cancelled…

There was a tapping at the French windows leading out

to the garden. She looked round. The nanny was there, smiling politely, with Georgy in his buggy. The nanny, Lyn now realised bleakly, Timon had hired to take her place.

How she got rid of her Lyn didn't know, but she did somehow. Somehow, too, she made herself go upstairs, walk into the bedroom she'd shared with Anatole and gaze down blindly at the bed where he'd taken her into his arms so often. She found her vision blurring, her throat burning.

She made herself look away, go to the closet, pick out the largest handbag she possessed. She put into it all the changes of clothes that she could cram in and, far more importantly, her passport, credit card and what little money she possessed. Then she went into Georgy's room and packed his bag with nappies and two changes of outfit, his favourite toys. Then, still with her vision blurred and her throat burning, she made herself go downstairs again, scoop him up and hug him tight, tight, *tight*…

With the shawl she had brought downstairs with her she made a makeshift sling and fitted him in the crook of her shoulder, awkwardly hefting the two bags onto her other shoulder. Her shoes were stout walking shoes and she needed them, for when she went outdoors she headed to the boundary of Timon Petranakos's property, scrambling over the rocky outcrop there precariously with her precious burden and then, on the other side, gaining the track that led up from the seashore to the main road, running east to west about a quarter of a kilometre inland. There, she knew, was a bus stop. From there she could take the bus to the nearby seaside town and then pick up a tram. The tram would take her where she so desperately, urgently needed to get to.

Piraeus, the port of Athens. Her gateway to escape…

It was crowded when she got there—crowded, busy and confusing. But she made herself decipher the notices,

found the ferry she wanted—the one that was the safest—
and bought a ticket with her precious store of euros. She
would not risk a credit card. That could be traced...

She hurried aboard the ferry, head down, Georgy in
her arms, trying not to look anxious lest she draw attention to herself. The ferry was bound for Crete. If she could
lie low there for a while, and then somehow—anyhow!—
get a flight back from Crete to the UK she could lie low
again, consult a family lawyer...do something that might
stop her losing Georgy.

*Will I have any chance now even to be his foster-carer?
What will happen now that Anatole isn't marrying me after
all? What happens to the adoption application?*

Questions, questions, questions—multiple and terrifying! Timon would make a move to claim Georgy, and
surely Anatole would too? She had to get to a lawyer, find
out what chance she had herself.

But, however puny her hopes, one thing was for sure—
if she stayed here in Greece then the long, powerful arm
of the Petranakos dynasty would easily overpower her!
Georgy would be ripped from her and she would stand
no chance—no chance at all—against what Timon and
Anatole could throw at her, with all their wealth and in-
fluence behind them.

*I have to get back to the UK! At least there I stand a
chance, however frail...*

Her mind raced on, churning and tumultuous, trying to
think, think, *think*, trying to keep her terror at bay.

Trying to keep at bay something that was even worse
than the terror.

It stabbed at her like a knife plunging deep into her.

Pain. Pain such as she had never known before. Pain that
savaged her like a wolf with a lamb in its tearing jaws. That
made her want to hunch over and rock with the agony of it.

She stumbled forward, gaining the seating area in the bow of the ferry, collapsing on one of the benches in the middle section, settling Georgy on her lap. He was staring about delightedly, fascinated by this new environment. She stared blindly out over the busy, crowded harbour, feeling a jolt as the ferry disengaged from the dock and started its journey. She willed it on faster, though she knew it would take until morning to reach Heraklion in Crete. She tried to think ahead, plan in detail what she would do once she arrived there, but her mind would not focus. The wind picked up as they reached the open sea, buffeting her where she sat exposed, feeling the savage jaws of pain tearing at her.

Anatole's name on the paper Timon had so triumphantly thrust at her.

Anatole's name betraying her.

His message to her confirming his betrayal.

His breaking of all the stupid trust she had put in him!

Her mind cried silently in anguish. *I trusted him! I trusted everything he said—everything he promised me!*

But it had meant nothing, that promise. Only one thing had mattered to him—getting Georgy to his grandfather and thereby getting control of the Petranakos Corporation.

And if that promise had meant nothing to him... Her eyes stared blindly, haunted, pained. Nor had anything else...

The stabbing pain came again. *Nothing about me mattered to him! Nothing!*

Like a film playing at high speed in her head all the time she had spent with Anatole flashed past her inner vision. Their time together with Georgy...

I thought we were making a family together! I thought he was happy to be with Georgy and me, happy for us to be together.

Being with her when Georgy slept...

Anatole's arms around her, his mouth seeking hers, his strong, passionate body covering hers, taking her to a paradise she had never known existed! Murmuring words to her, cradling her, caressing her...

But it had meant nothing at all—only as a means to lull her, to deceive her as to his true intentions. She heard his voice tolling in her head. Over and over again he'd said those words to her.

'Trust me—I need you to trust me...'

Bitter gall rose in her. Yes, he'd needed her to trust him! Needed her to gaze at him adoringly and put her trust in him, her faith in him.

Like a fool...

She heard his words again, mocking her from the depths of her being. She had meant nothing to him. Nothing more than a means to an end—to get Georgy out here the quickest and easiest way.

To get him here and keep him here.

Keep him here without her.

He lied to me...

But he had not been the only one to lie.

Like a crushing weight the accusation swung into her, forcing her to face it. She did not want to—she rebelled against it, resisted it—but it was impossible to deny, impossible to keep out of her head. It forced its way in, levering its way into her consciousness.

The brutal accusation cut at her. *You lied to him too—you lied to him and you knew that you were lying to him.*

And it was true—she *had* lied...lied right from the start...

Sickness filled her as she heard Timon's scathing denunciation of her—heard him telling her that she had got nothing but her just deserts...

A ragged breath razored through her as she stared out to

sea, the wind buffeting her face, whipping away her tears even as she shed them. But even as the wind sheared her tears away they fell faster yet. Unstoppable.

CHAPTER ELEVEN

ANATOLE RAISED A weary hand—a gesture of acknowledgement of what the union rep had just said. He was exhausted. His whole body was tired. He'd gone without sleep all night, going over and over figures and facts with the management team at the Thessaloniki plant, trying to find a viable alternative to the redundancies. Then he'd gone straight into meetings with the union representatives, trying to hammer out something that would preserve jobs.

At least he was making some kind of impact on the union. They were listening to him, even if they were still disputing with him. His approach was not that of the former manager, or his autocratic grandfather, issuing to the employees lofty diktats that had resulted in an instant demonstration outside the plant and ballots for full strike action. Instead he had disclosed the true finances of the division, pulled no punches, inviting them to try and find a way forward with him.

He sat back, weariness etched into his face. There was still muted discussion around the table. He wanted to close his eyes and sleep, but sleep could wait. It would have to. Would the deal he was offering swing it? He hoped so. Strike action would be costly and crippling, benefitting no one. Worse, in the terrifyingly volatile Greek economy it was likely to spread like wildfire through the rest of the

Petranakos organisation, possibly even beyond, to other companies as well, with disastrous consequences.

To his intense relief the union reps were looking thoughtful, and a couple of them were nodding. Had he swung it? He hoped to God he had—then maybe he could get some sleep finally.

But not before speaking to Lyn. It was imperative he do so! He'd managed to find the time to text her about the cancellation of the wedding, but that brief text was utterly inadequate. He had to see her, talk to her, explain to her…

Frustration knifed through him. He had to sleep, or he'd pass out, but he had to talk to her too. Had to get back to her…

'Kyrios Telonidis—'

The voice at the door of the meeting room was apologetic, but the note of urgency in it reached him. He looked enquiringly at the secretary who had intruded.

'It is Kyrios Petranakos…' she said.

He was on his feet immediately. 'Gentlemen—my apologies. My grandfather…' He left the sentence unfinished as he strode from the room. It was common knowledge how very gravely ill Timon was. In the outer office he seized the phone the secretary indicated. As he heard his grandfather's distinctive voice his tension diminished. He had feared the worst. But then, as he heard what his grandfather was saying, he froze.

'She's gone! She's gone—taken the boy! She's taken the boy!' It was all his grandfather could say, over and over again. Totally distraught.

'What did you say to her? Tell me what you said to her!'

Anatole's voice was harsh, but he needed to know what it was that had sent Lyn into a panic, making her flee as she had. Taking Georgy with her…

Since the call had come through to him in Thessa-

loniki life had turned into a nightmare. He had flown
straight back to Athens, raced to Timon's villa, stormed
into Timon's room.

His grandfather's face was ravaged.

'I told her what you'd done!'

Anatole's eyes flashed with fury. 'I told you to let *me*
tell her! That I would find the right way to say it! I knew
I needed to—urgently—but with that damn strike threatening I had to tell her to wait for me to talk to her! Why
the hell did you go and do it?'

He wasn't being kind, he knew that, but it was Timon's
fault! Timon's fault that Lyn had bolted. *Bolted with
Georgy!* He felt fear clutch at him. Where were they?
Where had Lyn gone? Where had she taken Georgy? They
could be anywhere! Anywhere at all! She'd taken her passport, and Georgy's, but even with his instant alerting of
the police at the airport there had been no reports of them.
His face tightened. Athens Airport was not the only way
out of Greece—there were a hundred ways she could have
gone...a hundred ways she could have left Greece!

'Why?' Timon's rasping voice was as harsh as his. *'This
is why!'* He seized a piece of paper from his desk, thrust
it at Anatole.

Anatole snatched it, forcing his eyes to focus, to take
in what he was reading. It was Latin script, in English.

As he read it he could feel ice congeal in his veins. He
let the paper fall back on the desk, staring down at it with
sightless eyes.

Beside him he could hear his grandfather's voice speaking. Coming from very far away.

'She lied to you—she lied to you and used you. Right from
the start! So I told her—I told her exactly what you'd done.'

Lyn was pushing Georgy around a park. The buggy was
not the swish, luxury item Anatole had bought. This one

was third-hand from a jumble sale, with a wonky wheel, a stained cover and a folding mechanism that threatened to break every time she used it. But it was all she could afford now. She was living off her savings. Getting any kind of work was impossible, because it would never be enough to cover childcare.

She'd found a bedsit—the cheapest she could get—a single room with a kitchenette in a corner and a shared bathroom on the landing, so cramped and run down it made the flat she'd lived in while at college seem like a luxury penthouse! Whenever she stared round it, taking in every unlovely detail, a memory flashed into her head.

The beautiful colour photo from the estate agent that had come with the title deeds to the seaside house in the Witterings in Sussex...

Her expression darkened. She had thought in her criminal stupidity that it was a gesture of Anatole's generous sensitivity to her plea that Georgy should not lose his English heritage...

She knew now what it really was—had known from the moment Timon had destroyed all her stupid dreams.

It was my payoff.

Well, she wouldn't touch it! Wouldn't take it! Would take nothing at all from him! She'd left all her expensive new clothes in the wardrobe in Timon's beach house, leaving Greece in her own, original clothes. Clothes that were far more suited to the place she lived now.

Yet even taking the cheapest bedsit she'd been able to find was eating into her funds badly. She could not continue like this indefinitely. She knew with a grim, bleak inevitability that a time of reckoning was approaching—heading towards her like a steam train. The knowledge was like a boot kicking into her head. She could not go on like this...

And not just because she would eventually run out of money.

But because she'd run off with Georgy.

Run from the man who was trying to take him from her! The man she had trusted never to do that.

Pain knifed her. Pain that was so familiar now, so agonising, that she should surely be used to it? But it was still like a stab every time she felt it—every time she thought of Anatole. Every time she remembered him.

Being with him—being in his arms! Being with him by day and by night! All the time we spent together—all the weeks—all that precious, precious time...

She closed her eyes, pushing the buggy blindly around the little park that was not too far away from the shabby bedsit she'd taken here in Bristol, which had been the destination of the first flight out of Heraklion. As she walked, forcing one foot in front of the other, memories rushed into her head, tearing at her with talons of sharpest steel. Memories of Anatole walking beside her in another city park like this, in the cold north country spring, sitting down by the children's play area. She heard his voice speaking in her head.

'There is a way,' he'd said. 'There is a way that could solve the entire dilemma...'

Her hands spasmed over the buggy's push bar. Yes, there had been a way to solve it! A way that he'd had all worked out—in absolute detail. Totally foolproof detail...

He had known—dear God—a man like him must have known from the off that she would be putty in his hands! That he could persuade her, convince her into doing what he wanted her to do!

'I need you to trust me...'

The words that she had heard him say so often to her burned like fire in her head.

And what better way to win her trust, keep her doting and docile, than by the most foolproof method of all...?

He took me to bed to get me to trust him. Just to keep me sweet.

Until he did not need to any more.

Her heart convulsed and she gave a little cry, pausing in her pushing and hunkering down beside Georgy. He turned to look at her and patted her face, gazing at her. She felt her heart turn over and over.

I love you so much! I love you so much, my darling, darling Georgy!

Yet as she straightened again, went on pushing forward, she felt as if a stone inside was dragging at her. She could not go on like this.

The harsh, brutal truth was that, though she had panicked when Timon had smashed her life to pieces, had followed every primal instinct in her body and fled as fast and as far as she could with Georgy in her arms, she was now on the run.

Hiding not just from Anatole and Timon but from the authorities in whose ultimate charge her sister's son still was...

It could not go on. She knew it—feared it—must face it.

Face, too, against the resistance that had cost her so much to overcome, that she was also hiding from the truth. The truth of what *she'd* done...

I used him too.

That was what she had to face—what Timon had thrown at her. Her own lie—her own deceit to get from Anatole what she wanted so desperately.

But it had all fallen apart—everything—and now she was reduced to this. Fleeing with Georgy—on the run—with no future, no hope.

It could not go on. There was only one way forward now. Only one future for Georgy.

If you love him, you must do it. For his sake!

In her head she heard the words she had cried out so often.

I can't do it! I can't—I can't! Lindy gave him to me with her dying words...Georgy is mine—mine!

But as she plodded on through the scruffy urban park that was a million miles away from the Petranakos mansion, with its huge private grounds and pristine private beach, her eyes staring wildly ahead of her, her face stark, she could feel the thoughts forcing their way into her tormented mind as desperately as she tried to keep them out.

They would not be kept out.

You must not think of yourself—your own pain, your own feelings! What you must think of is Georgy! If you love him, then do what is best for him!

He could not go on living like this, in some run down bedsit, hand to mouth. Hiding and on the run. Being fought over like a bone between two dogs in a cruel, punishing tug-of-love.

Slowly, as if she had no strength left in her, she wheeled the buggy around and headed back out of the park.

She had a letter to write.

Anatole walked into the air-conditioned building that housed the London offices of his lawyers. It hardly needed air-conditioning, because the London summer was a lot cooler than the Greek summer, but the temperature was the last thing he was thinking of. He had only one thought in his mind—only one imperative. He gave his name at the desk and was shown in immediately.

'Is she here?' was his instant demand to the partner who handled his affairs as he greeted him in his office.

The man nodded. 'She's waiting for you in one of our meeting rooms,' he said.

'And the boy?'

'Yes.'

The single word was all Anatole needed to hear. Relief flooded through him. It flushed away the other emotion that was possessing him—the one he was trying to exorcise with all his powers, which had possessed him ever since that fateful call from Timon.

'Do you wish me to be present at the meeting?' his lawyer enquired tactfully.

Anatole gave a curt shake of his head. 'I'll call you when I need you. You've outlined my legal position clearly enough, so I know where I stand.' He paused, not quite meeting the man's eyes. 'Did she say anything to you?'

The lawyer shook his head.

Anatole felt another stab of emotion go through him. He tensed his shoulders. 'OK, show me in.'

He blanked his mind. Anything else right now was far too dangerous. He must focus on only one goal—Georgy.

Nothing else.

No one else.

Lyn was sitting in one of the leather tub chairs that were grouped around a low table on which were spread several of the day's broadsheet newspapers, a copy of a business magazine and a law magazine. Georgy was on her lap, and she was nuzzling him with a soft toy. It was one of the ones that she and Anatole had bought for him in London, at the very expensive department store and with Aladdin's Cave of a toy department. It seemed they had bought it a lifetime ago—in a different universe.

She wondered what she was feeling right now and realised it was nothing. Realised that it had to be nothing—because if it were anything else she could not go on sitting there.

Waiting for Anatole to walk in, as she knew he would at any moment now.

There was a clock on the wall and she glanced at it. Time was ticking by. In a few minutes she would see him again, and then she would say to him what she must say.

But she must not think about that. Must only go on sitting here, absently playing with Georgy, while the minutes between her and her endless empty future ticked past.

The door opened. Her head jerked up and he was there. Anatole.

Anatole.

Here—now—in the flesh. Real. Live.

Anatole.

As overwhelming and as overpowering to her senses as he always had been, right from the very first...

The nothing she had been feeling shattered into a million fragments...

Like a tidal wave emotion roared into her, the blood in her veins gushing like a hot fountain released from a cave of ice. Her sight dimmed and her eyes clung to him as he walked in.

On her lap, Georgy saw him too—saw him, recognised him, and held out his chubby arms to him with a gurgle of delight.

In two strides Anatole was there, scooping him up, wheeling him into the air, folding him to him and hugging him, a torrent of Greek coming from his lips. Then, as he nestled Georgy into his shoulder, he turned to Lyn.

For a moment—just a moment—there was a flash of emotion in his eyes. It seemed to sear her to the quick. Then it was gone.

He stood stock-still, Georgy clutched to him, his face like stone. But she could feel his anger coming off him. Feel it spearing her.

'So you brought him. I did not think you would.' His voice had no expression in it.

She made herself answer. 'I said in my letter I would.' Her voice was halting. As expressionless as his. It was the only way she could make herself speak. Say the words she had to say.

He frowned a moment, his eyes narrowing. 'So why did you? Why did you bring him here? What are you after, Lyn?'

She heard the leashed anger and knew that *she* had caused it. But his anger didn't matter. She gave a faint, frail shrug. 'What else could I do? I ran, Anatole, because I panicked. It was instinct—blind, raw instinct—but once I was back here I realised there had been no point in running. No point in fleeing.' She looked at him. Made herself look at him. Made herself silence the scream inside her head against what she was doing. What she was saying. What she was feeling…

What you feel doesn't matter. Seeing Anatole again doesn't matter. It doesn't matter because you never mattered to him—you were just an impediment, in his way, a stepping stone towards his goal. It wasn't real, what happened between you. You were nothing to him but a means to an end. An end he has now achieved.

She looked at him holding Georgy, the baby sitting content in Anatole's arms. She had seen them like that a hundred times—a thousand. She felt her heart crash.

You were nothing to him—Georgy is everything!

And that was what she must cling to now. That and that alone. It was the only way to survive what was happening. What was going to happen.

'I thought,' he bit out, 'you might have gone to the house.'

She frowned. 'House? What house?'

A strange look flitted across his face. 'The house by the sea—the house I gave you.'

She stared. 'Why would I have gone there?' Her voice was blank.

'Because it's yours,' he riposted flatly. But the flatness was the flatness of the blade of a knife...

'Of course it isn't mine! Nothing's mine, Anatole. Not even—' She closed her eyes, because the truth was too agonising to face, then forced them open again. 'Not even Georgy.'

There—she had said it. Said what she had to say. What she should have said right from the start.

If I had just admitted it—admitted the truth—then I would have been spared all this now! Spared the agony of standing here, seeing Anatole, knowing what he came to mean to me!

Dear God, how much heartache she would have saved herself!

She took another breath that cut at her lungs, her throat, like the edge of a razorblade.

'I'll sign whatever paperwork needs to be signed,' she said. 'I can do it now or later—whatever you want. I'll have an address at some point. Though I don't know where yet.'

As she spoke she made herself stand up. Forced her legs to straighten. She felt faint, dizzy, but she had to speak— had to say what she had come to say.

She took a breath. Forced herself to speak.

'I've brought his things—Georgy's. There isn't much. I didn't take much with me. And I've only bought a little more here in the UK. It's all in those bags.' She indicated the meagre collection on the floor by the chair. 'The buggy isn't very good—it's from a jumble sale—but it's just about useable until you get a new one. Unless you brought his old one with you... Be careful when you unfold it, it catches—' She pointed to where it was propped up against the wall.

She fumbled in her bag. Her fingers weren't working properly. Nothing about her was working properly.

'Here is his passport,' she said, and placed it on the little table. There was the slightest tremble in her voice, but she fought it down. She must not break—she *must* not… 'I hope—' she said. 'I hope you can take him back to Greece as quickly as possible. I am sure…' She swallowed. 'I'm sure Timon must want to see him again as soon as he can.'

Her voice trailed off. She picked up her bag, blinked a moment.

'I think that's everything,' she said.

She started to walk to the door. She must not look at Anatole. Must not look at Georgy. Must do absolutely nothing except keep walking to the door. Reach it, start to open it…

'What the *hell* are you doing?'

The demand was like a blow on the back of her neck. She turned. Swallowed. It was hard to swallow because there was a rock the size of Gibraltar in her throat. She blinked again.

'I'm going,' she said. 'What did you think I would do?'

He said something. Something she did not catch because she was looking at his face. Looking at his face for the very last time. Knowing that it was the very last time was like plunging her hand into boiling water. But even as she looked his expression changed.

'So he was right.' The words came low, with a lash that was like a whip across her skin. 'Timon was right all along.'

Slowly he set Georgy down on the thickly carpeted floor, pulling off his tie to keep him happy. Lyn found her eyes going to the strong column of his neck as he unfastened the top button of his shirt now that he was tieless. Felt the ripple in her stomach that was oh, so familiar— and now so eviscerating.

'Timon was right,' he said again. His voice was Arctic. 'He said you only wanted money out of all of this! I didn't believe him. I said you'd turned down cash from me to hand over Georgy. But he read you right all along!' His voice twisted. 'No wonder he set his private investigators on to you—and no wonder you took his money to clear out!'

She didn't answer. Only picked up Georgy's passport. Thrust it at him.

'Open it,' she said. Her voice was tight. As tight as the steel band around her throat, garrotting her.

She watched him do as she had demanded. Watched his expression change as he saw Timon's uncashed cheque within, torn into pieces.

'I took it from him to give me time to make my escape. Because I could think of nothing else to do.' She took a ragged shredded breath. 'I never wanted money, Anatole,' she told him. 'I never wanted anything except one thing—the one thing that was the most precious in my life.'

Her eyes dropped to Georgy, happily chewing on Anatole's silk tie.

She was lying, she knew. Lying because she'd come to want more than Georgy—to want something even more precious to her.

You! You, Anatole—I wanted you so much! And a family—you, and Georgy and me—I wanted that so much! So much!

That had been the dream that had taken shape in Greece—that had made her heart catch with yearning! Anatole and Georgy and her—a family together...

She lifted her eyes to Anatole again. To his blank, expressionless face.

'I kept telling you Georgy was mine,' she said. 'I said it over and over and over again. As if by saying it I might make it true.' She stopped. Took a razoring breath that cut at the soft tissue of her lungs. Then said what she had to say. *Had* to say.

'But he isn't mine. He never was.'

She looked at Anatole—looked straight at him. Met his hard, masked gaze unflinchingly as she made her damning confession.

'Not a drop of my blood runs in his veins.'

CHAPTER TWELVE

ANATOLE'S FACE WAS stark. Hearing Lyn say what he now knew…

'I know that now,' he said. His voice was strange, but he kept on speaking all the same. 'I know that Lindy wasn't your sister. She wasn't even your half-sister. She was nothing more than your stepsister. Timon showed me what his investigators found. She was the daughter of your mother's second husband, who left her with your mother and you when he abandoned the marriage—*and* his daughter.'

He shook his head as if he were shaking his thoughts into place—a new place they were unaccustomed to.

'When he told me it made such sense. Why Georgy doesn't look like you. Why your name is so similar to Lindy's—no parent would have done that deliberately—and why I sometimes caught that look of fear in your eyes. Like when you didn't want a DNA test done.' He paused. 'Why didn't you tell me, Lyn? You must have known I would find out at some point?'

She gave a laugh. A bitter, biting laugh.

'Because I wanted to be married to you before you did!' she cried. 'I was scheming to get your ring on my finger—the ring you never intended to put there!'

His expression changed. He opened his mouth to speak but she ploughed on. 'Timon told me! He told me that the whole damn thing had been nothing more than a ruse! All that stuff about getting married to strengthen our joint claim to adopt Georgy between us! All that was a fairy tale! You never meant a word of it!'

'What?' The word broke from him explosively.

She put her hands to her ears. 'Anatole—don't! Please—don't! Don't lie to me now—we're done with lies! We're done with them!' That brief, bitter laugh came again. It had no humour in it, only an ocean of pain, and she let her hands fall to her sides. 'Timon threw it at me that I deserved everything I was ending up with because I'd lied to you by not telling you that Lindy was only my stepsister. I knew perfectly well that your claim to Georgy would be stronger than mine ever could be! Because you were a blood relative and I wasn't! I was trying to trap you into a marriage you never needed to make!'

She threw her head back.

'When he tried to give me money to leave, told me he knew I only wanted to marry you because you were rich, I was angry! I've never wanted your money—*never*! I only wanted Georgy!'

She took a shuddering breath, shaking her head as if the knowledge of what she had done was too heavy a weight to carry. 'But none of it matters now. It's over. I know that—I've accepted it. I've accepted everything. And I've accepted most of all that I have to do what I am doing now.'

Her eyes went to Georgy again, so absolutely and utterly unaware of the agonising drama above his head.

'I called him mine,' she whispered. The words would hardly come, forced through a throat that was constricted with grief. 'But he never was. He was never mine. Only my stepsister's baby. Your cousin's son. Which is why…'

She lifted her eyes again, made them go to Anatole, who was standing like a statue, frozen. She felt her heart turn over. Turn over uselessly in her heart.

'Which is why,' she said again, and her voice was dead

now, 'I'm leaving him. He isn't a bone to be fought over,
or a prize, or a bequest, or anything at all except himself.
He needs a home, a family—*his* family. *Your* family. You'll
look after him. I know you will. And you love him—I
know you love him. And I know that Timon loves him too,
in his own way.' She took a heavy razoring breath that cut
into her lungs. 'I should have seen that from the start—that
I had no claim to him. Not once you had found him. He's
yours, Anatole—yours and Timon's. It's taken till now for
me to accept that. To accept that I should never have put
you through what I have. I see that now.'

She picked up her bag. It seemed as heavy as lead. As
heavy as the millstone grinding her heart to chaff.

'I won't say goodbye to Georgy. He's happy with you.
That's all that counts.' Her voice was odd, she noticed with
a stray, inconsequential part of her brain.

She turned away, pulling open the door. Not looking
back.

An iron band closed around her arm, halting her in
her tracks. Anatole was there, pulling her back, slamming
the door shut, holding her with both hands now, clamped
around her upper arms.

'Are you insane?' he said. 'Are you completely insane?
You cannot seriously imagine you are just going to walk
out like that?'

She strained away from him, but it was like straining
against steel bonds. He was too close. Far, far too close. It
meant she could see everything about him. The strong wall
of his chest, the breadth of his shoulders sheathed in the expensive material of his handmade suit, the line of his jaw,
darkening already, see the sculpted mouth that could skim
her body and reduce her to soft, helpless cries of passion.

She could see the eyes that burned with dark gold fire.

Catch the scent of his body.

See the black silk of his lashes.

She felt faint with it.

She shut her eyes to block the vision. Stop the memories. The memories that cut her like knives on softest flesh.

'What else is there to do?' she said. Her voice was low and strained. 'You don't want to marry me—you've never wanted to marry me—and Timon doesn't want you to marry me. He made that clear enough! And now you're not marrying me I can do what Timon told me to do—clear off and leave you alone. Leave Georgy alone, too. Because he doesn't need me. He's got you, he's got Timon, he's got everything he needs. The nanny will look after him while you're at work. She's very good, I'm sure. He doesn't need me and he won't remember me—he won't miss me.'

'And Georgy is the only person you're concerned about? Is that it?' There was still something odd about Anatole's voice, but she wouldn't think about that. Wouldn't think about anything. Wouldn't *feel* anything.

Dared not.

She opened her eyes again, made herself look at him. 'No,' she said. She stepped back and this time he let her go. She took another step, increasing the distance between them. The distance was more than physical—far, far more. 'There's you, too,' she said.

She made herself speak. 'I'm sorry I put you through so much anxiety—running away from Greece as I did—but at the time I was still…still in denial. Still thinking I had a right to Georgy. And that made me so…so angry with you.' She picked the word *angry* because it was the only safe one to use. Any of the other words—*anguished*, *agonised*, *distraught*—were all impossible to use. Quite impossible! 'Because I trusted you—just like you kept telling me to trust you—when you said you would make it all work out. That if we married we'd have a much better chance of adopting Georgy.'

She took another heaving breath, and now the words broke from her.

'But all along you were just telling me that in order to get me to agree to bring Georgy out to Greece. Because with me as his foster-carer it was the quickest way to get him there—me taking him—rather than going through the courts for permission on your own behalf. You knew I was fearful of bringing Georgy to Greece, so you spun me all that stuff about marrying and then divorcing. And to keep me sweet—'

She heard her voice choke but forced herself to speak, forced herself to say it all to voice every last agony.

'To keep me sweet you...you... Well, you did the obvious thing. And it worked—it worked totally. I actually believed you really were going to marry me—and I desperately wanted that to happen, because marrying you gave *me* my best chance to adopt Georgy!'

The words were pouring from her now, unstoppable.

'It's because I'm not a blood relation that that the authorities have always wanted him to be adopted by someone else! But then there was you—a close relation to his father—and being your wife would have been *my* best chance as well! That's why I did it, Anatole—that's why I agreed to marry you. And I've been well served. I have no claim to him and that's what I've finally accepted. Georgy isn't mine and never was—never will be!'

As her gaze clung to the man standing there—the man she had given herself to, the man who meant so much to her, who had caused her such anguish—she heard her mind whisper the words that burned within her head.

And nor are you mine! You aren't mine and never were—never will be! I'll never see you again after today—never! And my heart is breaking—breaking for Georgy... Breaking for you.

It *was* breaking. She knew it—could feel it—could feel

the fractures tearing it apart, tearing *her* apart as she spoke, as she looked upon him for the very last time in her life… The man she had fallen in love with so incredibly stupidly! So rashly and foolishly! She had fallen in love with him when to him she was only a means to an end—a way to get hold of the child he'd so desperately sought with the least fuss and the most speed!

She took another harrowing breath. 'So I can finally do what I know I have to do—walk away and leave Georgy to you. Because you love him and you will care for him all his life. He won't need me—I can see that clearly now… quite, quite clearly.'

'Can you?' Again he seemed only to echo her words.

She nodded. Her eyes were wide and anguished, but she made herself say the words she had to say. Say them to Anatole. The man who would be Georgy's father—she would never, *never* be his mother!

'Like I said, I accept now that he doesn't need me. He has you, Anatole, and that is enough. You'll be a wonderful father! You love him to pieces, and he adores you. *And* your silk ties,' she added.

But she mustn't attempt humour—not even as a safety valve. Emotion of any kind now was far too dangerous. Being here in this room, with Anatole and Georgy, was far too dangerous. She had to go now, while she still could…

'You can't see straight at *all*! You can't even see what's right in front of you!'

Anatole's harsh voice cut across her. Then it changed.

'But I can understand why.' He took a ragged breath. 'I can understand everything now.'

He reached forward, took her wrist. Drew her away from the door towards the group of chairs. He sat her down in one, and himself in the other. She went without resistance. Her limbs were not her own suddenly.

Georgy, still on the carpet, seeing her close by, started

to crawl towards her, a happy grin on his face. He reached her leg and clung to it with chubby arms. Her face worked.

'Pick him up, Lyn,' said Anatole.

She shook her head.

'I can't,' she said. 'I mustn't—he isn't mine.'

Her throat was aching, as if every tendon was stretched beyond bearing.

Anatole leant down, scooped up Georgy, put him on Lyn's lap.

'Hold him,' he told her.

There was something wrong with his voice again. It was harsh and hoarse.

'Hold him and look at me. Tell me again what you've just said. That you are going to walk out on Georgy. Abandon him.'

A vice closed over her heart, crushing it. 'I'm…I'm not abandoning him. I'm…I'm doing what is right. What has to be done. What I should have done from the moment you first found him. He isn't mine. He never was mine.…'

Her throat closed again but she made herself go on, made herself lift her stricken gaze to the dark eyes that were boring into her like drills…

'I should have given him to you straight away—when you first came to me! Then you would never have had to go through that charade, that farce—the one your grandfather called time on. The one…' She swallowed. 'The one that you were just about to end yourself away.' She looked at him, her gaze heavy as lead. 'I got a phone call from the town hall after Timon had spoken to me—a phone call confirming that the wedding had been cancelled. And then…' She swallowed again. 'Then I got your text, telling me the same thing.'

'In that text I told you I would *explain everything* when I spoke to you later!'

Anatole's voice seared her.

'Timon had already made everything clear to me—and when I tried not to believe him he set me straight too. He showed me the document you'd signed—the one giving you the chairmanship of the Petranakos Corporation, the one affirming that you would not be marrying me. So what would have been the point, Anatole, in you telling me that yourself when I had it in writing already?'

Greek words spat from him.

Lyn's gaze slid away, down to the baby sitting on her lap, placidly chewing on Anatole's tie, content just to be on her knees. She wanted to put her arms around him but she must not. Not any more.

Anatole was speaking again and she made herself listen—though what could he say that she could want to hear?

'The *point*, Lyn,' he bit out, and each word was cut like a diamond from the air, 'was that *I* would have told you the truth!'

'I knew the truth,' she answered. 'Timon told me.'

'Timon,' said Anatole carefully—very carefully, 'lied.'

Lyn's eyes went to his. There was still that dull blankness in them. Why was he saying this? What for?

'I saw the document you signed,' she said. 'I saw it in the English translation and I saw the original—the one in Greek with your signature on it. I translated it myself. It said what Timon told me it said. You are the new chairman and you won't be marrying me.'

'And did it tell you *why*?'

There was still that strangeness in his voice. She heard it, but knew she must not...

'Timon told me why. Because you never intended to marry me. It was all a ruse, to get me to agree to bring Georgy out to Greece.'

'Well,' he said, speaking in the same clear, careful voice, as if she were hard of learning, 'in that case why didn't I just put you on the first flight back to London once Georgy was in Athens?'

She gave a shrug. 'I don't know. It doesn't matter.'

It didn't matter. Not now. Not now that everything she had hoped and dreamed was smashed to pieces. Not now when her heart was breaking—breaking twice over. For Georgy and for Anatole.

Georgy was looking up at her and absently she stroked his hair. It felt like silk beneath her fingers.

I'll never hold him again on my lap. Never hug him or kiss him. Never see him grow up...

Her eyes went to Anatole, standing there—so very dear to her, so very precious.

And she had never mattered to him at all...

Pain curdled around her heart. She wished he would stop talking to her, stop asking her things—things that did not matter that could not matter ever again. But he was talking again. Still talking at her—like some nightmare *post mortem*...

'Yes, Lyn—it *does* matter. Why would I want you to stay on in Greece, live with me in the beach house, sleep with me, if I'd already got what I wanted from you?'

Her brow furrowed. He was going on at her and there wasn't any point—*there wasn't any point!*

'Well, maybe it was because I might still have come in useful for some reason or other! You might have found it helpful to have me on side when you applied to adopt Georgy. I'd be kept sweet and not contest you.' Her voice changed. 'Only that wouldn't have been necessary, would it? Once you knew I was only Lindy's stepsister, it meant I wouldn't stand a chance of fighting you for Georgy. Then you could have—*would* have—done exactly what your grandfather did. Sent me packing!'

He looked at her. 'Do you know why he sent you packing, Lyn?'

It was clear to him now—crystal clear. But she couldn't see it yet. He had to show it to her.

She shook her head dully. Anatole's eyes—his dark sloe eyes that could melt her with a single glance—rested on her.

'He was frightened, Lyn. Once he knew that Lindy was only your stepsister he was frightened that you were using me—using me to strengthen your own claim to Georgy. By marrying me you'd become his adoptive mother if our claim went through, whether you were his aunt or only his step-aunt. It would have been too late then. He was scared, Lyn—scared you'd take Georgy back to England, divorce me there, go for custody. Hold Georgy to ransom.' He paused. 'It was fear, Lyn, that made him say what he said to you.'

She shut her eyes. Why was he saying these things? It was a torment to her! 'And did he fake your signature on that document?' she demanded, her eyes flying open again. '*Did* he?'

Anatole shook his head. 'No—I signed it.' He paused. 'I had to. He gave me no choice.' His voice was steady. Controlled. *Very* controlled. 'I need you to listen to me, Lyn. I need you to hear what I am telling you. I would have told you in Greece, had you not run away.'

He took a heavy breath, keeping his relentless gaze on her. She was as white as a sheet, as tense as stretched wire.

'I signed that document,' he said, 'because Timon was refusing to hand over the chairmanship unless I did. And you know what the situation was in Thessaloniki. But I did not want to sign it.' He took another breath. 'I understand now, as I did not then, that the reason he insisted on my signing it was because he already knew about you and Lindy! He already had that report from his investigators—an investigation I knew nothing about. That is what scared him—and that is why he used the only leverage he had: threatening not to give me the power I needed so urgently, that very day, so that I could end that disastrous strike, unless I undertook not to marry you. I only found out about you being Lindy's stepsister when I rushed back to him from Thessaloniki—*after* you'd fled with Georgy! He told me then—told me and denounced you for taking the cheque he offered you. And *that* is why I've doubted you—*that* is why I was angry when I came here!'

'You had a right to be angry, Anatole—knowing I'd hidden from you how weak my claim to Georgy was compared to yours.' Her voice was the same—dull, self-accusing.

He stared at her. 'You think I am angry at you for *that*?'

'Just as I was angry,' she countered. 'Angry that you said we would marry but you never meant it. That document was proof of that!'

His expression changed. 'I would *never*,' he bit out, his eyes flashing darkly, 'have signed such a document of my own free will! But,' he said, 'I signed it in the end because I didn't think it mattered. Not in the long term. I didn't have time to argue with my grandfather. I didn't have time to debate the issue—question why he was insisting on that condition. I had to focus on what was going on in Thessaloniki! Afterwards I would sort it out! I'd have had to postpone the wedding anyway—because of the strike threatening—and if you'd given me a chance, Lyn, when I got back I would have explained what my grandfather had made me do, why I agreed to it! I would have explained *everything* to you.' He took a razoring breath. 'If you'd trusted me enough not to run away back to England…' His face worked. 'If you'd only trusted me, Lyn.'

'Trust me—I need you to trust me…'

The words he had said so often to her. And he was saying them again!

Emotion speared within her—emotion she could not name. Dared not name.

'Trusted me as I need you to trust me now.'

His voice came through the teeming confusion in her head.

'As I trust *you*, Lyn—as I trust you.'

He stepped towards her and she could only gaze at him—gaze into his face, his eyes, which seemed to be pouring into hers.

He levered himself down beside her, hunkering on his haunches. 'You have proved to me that I can have trust in you now, in the most absolute way possible! There is no greater proof possible! *None!*'

He reached a hand forward. But not to her. To Georgy, who was contentedly sucking at his fingers now, clearly getting sleepy. Anatole stroked his head and cupped his cheek, smoothed his hand down his back. His face softened. Then his gaze went back to Lyn. Clear and unflinching.

'I trust you, Lyn—absolutely and unconditionally. I trust you to do the one thing that shines from you, that has shone from you like a beacon of purest light from the very first!' His expression changed. 'Your love for Georgy, Lyn. *That* is what I trust—and it is why I trust you. Why I will *always* trust you!'

There was a wealth of emotion in his voice, pouring from his eyes, from his whole being. She felt herself sway with the force of it.

'What does it matter, Lyn, whether Lindy was your sister—?' he began.

But she cut across him, her voice a cry. Anguished and trembling with emotion. 'She *was*! She *was* my sister! My sister in *everything*! I loved her as just as much! And when she died a piece of me died as well. But she gave me—' her voice broke '—she gave me her son, for me to look after, to love the way I'd loved her. And that's why… that's why…' She couldn't go on. But she had to—she *had* to. 'That's why I have to give him to you now, Anatole—because it's for *him*.'

Now it was Anatole who cut across her. 'And *that* is why I know how much you love him! *Because* you are willing to give him up!' His voice changed, grew husky. 'And there is only one kind of love that does that, Lyn—only one kind.' He looked at her. 'A mother's love.' He took a shaking breath and swallowed. '*You* are Georgy's mother! *You!* And it doesn't matter a single iota whether your blood runs in his veins! Your sister knew that—knew that when she entrusted Georgy to you! She knew you loved her and she knew you would love Georgy all his life, Lyn—*all his life!* With the love he needs to have—a mother's love... *your* love!'

He reached forward again, and now he was taking her hands with his, so warm and so strong, and he was placing her hands around Georgy's sturdy little body, pressing them around him, his own covering hers.

'And I love him too, Lyn,' he said. 'I love him with the love that Marcos was not able to love him with. I will always love him—all his life.' He paused and took another ragged breath. 'Just as I love you, Lyn.'

There was a sudden stillness. An absolute stillness. An immobility of all the world. All the universe.

She could not move. Could not move a muscle.

But she could feel Anatole lifting her hands—lifting them away from Georgy, who slumped his slumberous body back against her, his eyelids closing. Anatole lifted her hands to his lips, kissing first one and then the other. The softest, sweetest kisses...

'How could you think I didn't?' he whispered. His voice was cracking—cracking and husky. 'How could you possibly think I didn't love you? How did you think I could hold you in my arms night after night, be with you, at your side day after day, and not come to love you as I do?'

Her eyes clung to his. Was this true? Oh, was this true? These words he was telling her? Those sweet kisses he had blessed her hands with? Was it true? Her heart swelled with hope—with yearning that it might be so—that she was really hearing him say those wonderful words she had so longed to hear and had thought could never be said by him.

But she *was* hearing them—hearing him say them—and feeling the blissful brush of his lips on hers, the glowing warmth of his gaze, his fingers winding into hers…

He was speaking still, saying what was bliss for her to hear. 'And I know—I *know*—you love me too! I can see it now—in your face, your eyes, your tears, Lyn, which are pouring down your face. You love Georgy and you love me—and I love Georgy and I love you. And that's all we need, my darling, darling Lyn—all that we will ever need!'

He reached with his mouth for hers and found it, kissed it, tasting the salt of her tears.

'All we'll ever need,' he said again, drawing away. He looked at her. 'You must never, never doubt me again. *Never!* To think that you thought so ill of me that you fled back here—that you felt you had to give up Georgy to me. To think that is like a sword in my side!' He kissed her again—fiercely, possessively. 'We are *family*, Lyn! Family. You and me and Georgy—and we always will be! *Always!*'

She swallowed, fighting back the longing to believe everything he was telling her. 'Our plan was to marry and then divorce,' she said. Her voice sounded wonky to her, the words coming out weirdly. It must be because there wasn't any room for them, she thought. There was only room for the tidal wave of emotion coursing through her—filling her being.

'That,' he answered her roundly, 'was the stupidest plan in the universe! What we are going to do is just marry. And stay married! For *ever*!'

'That document you signed…'

'Timon will tear it up—or I will do it for him!' He gave a ragged laugh. 'Timon will only have to take one look at us to know his fears are groundless—pointless.' His expression changed, and so did his voice, becoming sombre, worried. 'Can you forgive him, Lyn? For lying to you and saying that I never intended to marry you so that he could drive you away? It was fear that made him do what he did. I can see that now. The fear of losing Georgy.'

Her eyes shadowed. She knew what fear was. Knew it in her bones—knew the fear of losing Georgy…knew just what that fear could make one do…

She took a breath, looked at Anatole straight. 'I lied to you because I was so frightened I might lose Georgy,' she said, swallowing. 'I understand why Timon lied to me for the same reason.'

His hands tightened on hers. 'Thank you,' he said. His eyes were expressive. 'And I can tell you with absolute certainty that when he knows that we are to be a real family now he will be overjoyed!'

A little choke escaped her. 'Oh, God, Anatole—is it true? Is *any* of this true? I walked in here and my heart was breaking—breaking in two. Breaking at giving up Georgy, breaking because I love you so much and I thought you'd only used me and thrown me away! I can't believe this now—I can't believe this happiness I'm feeling! I can't *believe* it!'

Did she dare? Did she *dare* believe what Anatole was saying to her? Did she dare believe in the love pouring from his eyes…?

Believe in the love pouring from her heart…

There was only one answer he could give her. Only one answer, and she heard him say the words she had heard him speak so often.

'Lyn, I need you to trust me on this!' He took a ragged

breath. 'I need you to trust that I will love you for the rest of my days! Just—I *beg* you!—trust me!'

As he spoke, with his love for her pouring from his eyes, she felt the dam of her fears break—and all those hideous, nightmare fears that had convulsed and crucified her flowed away, emptying out of her, never to return.

And in their place blossomed the sweet and glorious flower of her love for Anatole—love given and received, each to the other.

Anatole! *Her* Anatole. And she was his—*his*! And she always would be. She would trust him now—for ever, in everything!

He kissed her again, sealing that love in tenderness and passion, with Georgy cradled in her lap, their arms around him. It was an endless kiss…interrupted by the sound of someone clearing his throat from the doorway. She and Anatole sprang apart.

'Oh,' said a surprised voice. 'Ah…' It fell silent.

Lyn bit her lip, looking down at Georgy, unable to look anywhere else. But Anatole got to his feet, slipping Lyn's hand from his but standing beside her, his hand resting on her shoulder warmly. Possessively.

The room was bathed in sunlight—which was odd. Because outside he could see that it was mizzling with the doleful rain of an English summer. Yet the air inside the room seemed golden with the sun…as golden as the happiness flooding through him.

He looked across at his lawyer. 'I think,' he said, 'we've just reached an out of court settlement.' His voice was very dry.

His lawyer's was even dryer. 'Well, I'll just leave you, then, to…ah…hammer out the details, shall I?'

'That,' said Anatole, and his hand pressed down on Lyn's shoulder, 'might take some time.'

He glanced at Lyn and his gaze was as warm as the love he felt for her. Her answering gaze was just as warm.

'It might take a lifetime,' he said.

EPILOGUE

LYN SETTLED BACK into the padded beach chair beneath a striped parasol. Beside her Timon, resplendent in a very grand wheelchair, sat smiling benevolently. A little way in front of both of them, on the beach in front of Timon's villa, was Anatole, in shorts and T-shirt in the late summer heat, sprawled on the sand with Georgy, showing him how to use a bucket and spade. Georgy, recklessly waving his own plastic spade in a manner likely to engage hard with Anatole's tousled head, was happily thumping at his upturned plastic bucket with enthusiastic dedication and muscular vigour.

'I thought you were supposed to be building a sand-castle,' Lyn called out, laughing.

It was good to see Anatole relaxing, having more time to do so. His dedicated attentions to the Petranokos empire had been successful, and it was on a much surer footing now, with all the employees' jobs secure, which allowed him to ease back significantly on his work schedule. Giving him far more time with his family.

With his adored Georgy.

And his adored bride.

They had married as soon as they had returned to Greece. Timon, enthroned in his wheelchair, had proved a benign and approving host for a wedding followed by a luxurious and leisurely honeymoon—with Georgy!—on a tour of the Aegean in the Petranakos yacht.

The honeymoon had been followed by a journey back to England to take possession of the seaside house in Sussex that Anatole had bought for Lyn. It would be their UK base for future visits and holidays. And they had attended, hand in in hand, their closeness and unity and their devotion to Georgy visible to the family court judge, the hearing of their application to adopt the baby they both loved as much as they loved each other. Their application had been approved, and now Georgy was theirs for ever.

Every day Lyn spent a considerable amount of time with Georgy and his great-grandfather—a lot of it here, on the beach that Georgy loved, with Timon's wheelchair shaded by an awning.

'We'll start on the sandcastle any minute now,' Anatole riposted. 'Once Georgy's got bored with hitting things!'

A low rumble of laughter came from Timon. Lyn glanced at him. He was looking healthy, considering… He was still doing well on the drugs, and it was buying him some time. The precious time he so desperately wanted.

As if he could sense her looking at him, Timon reached to take Lyn's hand and pat it affectionately with his own gnarled one. He turned his head to smile at her.

Though she had had some trepidation, they had made their peace.

'I wronged you,' he had told her. 'And from the bottom of my heart I apologise to you. It was fear that made me harsh—fear that you would take Marcos's son from us. But I know now that you would never do such a thing. For you love him as much as we do.' His voice had softened. 'And you love my grandson too. You will both, I know, be the parents that Marcos and your sister could not be. I know now,' he'd said, 'that Marcos's son is safe with you and always will be.'

It had been all she'd needed to hear. Just as now all she needed in the world was to be here, with her husband and their son, a family united in love. Tragedy had reached its dark shadows across them all, but now sunlight was strong and bright and warm in their lives.

Timon turned back to look at his grandson and Georgy.

'The years pass so swiftly,' he said. 'How short a time it seems since it was Anatole and Marcos playing on the beach. But I am blessed—so very blessed—to have been granted this, now.'

She squeezed his hand comfortingly. 'We are all blessed,' she said.

Unconsciously she slid a hand across her still-flat stomach. Timon caught the gesture. They had told him as soon as they had known themselves of Lyn's pregnancy. Timon needed all the reasons they could find to keep on fighting for his life. Another great-grandchild could only help that.

'A brother for Georgy,' he said approvingly.

'It might be a sister,' Lyn pointed out.

Timon shook his head decisively. 'He needs a younger brother,' he said. 'Someone he can look out for, just as Anatole looked out for Marcos. Someone to encourage him to be sensible and wise.'

She smiled peaceably—she was not about to argue. Whether girl or boy, the new baby would be adored, just as Georgy was, and that was all that mattered.

As if sensing he was being discussed, and in complimentary terms, Georgy ceased his thumping and grinned at all of them.

'Right, then, Georgy,' said Anatole briskly, '*this* is how we build a sandcastle.'

Georgy turned his eyes to his new father, gazed at him with grave attention and considerable respect—then hit him smartly on the head with his plastic spade, chortling gleefully as he did so.

'Oh, Georgy!' exclaimed Lyn ruefully. 'You little monster!'

* * * * *